"This must be...

Reece frowned as he... ...ssessed Zoe.

Claire tensed. This was the moment she'd played over and over in her head. The moment Zoe met her father. In her carefully orchestrated daydreams, she somehow imagined she'd be in control of the situation.

"Zoe, this is Mr. Reece."

Her daughter peeked out from behind Claire. She pushed a strand of hair from her eyes and stared at Reece, her dark blue eyes curious.

"Can you say hello?" Claire prompted.

"Hello."

"Hi, there." He knelt and offered Zoe a smile. "I'm thinking you're the same age as one of my nephews."

"I'm five," Zoe said proudly.

"Five, huh? Almost ready to start school."

"Uh-huh," Zoe said with a proud nod of her head.

Reece blinked as if processing the information. He stood and looked at Claire. Looked at her long and hard before he turned to Zoe again. A chill passed over Claire as she realized he was doing the math.

Not now, not here in front of Zoe. Please.

Tina Radcliffe has been dreaming and scribbling for years. Originally from Western New York, she left home for a tour of duty with the US Army Security Agency stationed in Augsburg, Germany, and ended up in Tulsa, Oklahoma. Her past careers include certified oncology RN, library cataloger and pharmacy clerk. She recently moved from Denver, Colorado, to the Phoenix, Arizona, area, where she writes heartwarming and fun inspirational romance.

Books by Tina Radcliffe

Love Inspired

Hearts of Oklahoma

Finding the Road Home
Ready to Trust

Big Heart Ranch

Claiming Her Cowboy
Falling for the Cowgirl
Christmas with the Cowboy
Her Last Chance Cowboy

The Rancher's Reunion
Oklahoma Reunion
Mending the Doctor's Heart
Stranded with the Rancher
Safe in the Fireman's Arms
Rocky Mountain Reunion
Rocky Mountain Cowboy

Visit the Author Profile page at Harlequin.com for more titles.

Ready to Trust

Tina Radcliffe

LOVE INSPIRED
INSPIRATIONAL ROMANCE

If you purchased this book without a cover you should be aware that this book is stolen property. It was reported as "unsold and destroyed" to the publisher, and neither the author nor the publisher has received any payment for this "stripped book."

LOVE INSPIRED®

INSPIRATIONAL ROMANCE

Recycling programs
for this product may
not exist in your area.

ISBN-13: 978-1-335-55380-5

Ready to Trust

Copyright © 2020 by Tina M. Radcliffe

All rights reserved. No part of this book may be used or reproduced in any manner whatsoever without written permission except in the case of brief quotations embodied in critical articles and reviews.

This is a work of fiction. Names, characters, places and incidents are either the product of the author's imagination or are used fictitiously. Any resemblance to actual persons, living or dead, businesses, companies, events or locales is entirely coincidental.

This edition published by arrangement with Harlequin Books S.A.

For questions and comments about the quality of this book, please contact us at CustomerService@Harlequin.com.

Love Inspired
22 Adelaide St. West, 40th Floor
Toronto, Ontario M5H 4E3, Canada
www.Harlequin.com

Printed in U.S.A.

It is of the Lord's mercies that we are not
consumed, because his compassions fail not.
They are new every morning:
great is thy faithfulness.
—*Lamentations* 3:22–23

A big thanks to wranglers Alysha Worthen and Heather Pickett for naming Tucker's twins, Hazel and Ginger. And to the lovely and humorous Ronda Tumberg for sharing the name Reece with me. I think all Reeces must be heroes.

Thank you to my editor, Dina Davis, who ensures that each book is better than the last by helping me to grow as a writer and putting up with my growing pains.

As always, thank you to my agent, Jessica Alvarez, who not only is in my corner but answers emails faster than a speeding bullet.

Finally, I thank the Lord for His unconditional love and all He has given me, especially Tom, Timothy, Michael, David and Amy.

Chapter One

Reece Rainbolt stepped into the Rebel, Oklahoma, law office of Edwin P. Sanders, Esquire. The scent of polished wood, new leather and fresh coffee stirred up memories of the last time he'd been in this particular office.

Sixteen years.

He'd just turned twenty-one, and his big brother Mitch had accompanied him to sign off on the paperwork that would grant him part ownership in Rebel Ranch. Fast forward sixteen years and Reece now managed his family's prospering guest ranch on the outskirts of town. These days he did all his legal business in Tulsa—far from the small-town gossip mill.

He removed his cowboy hat and nodded to the smiling middle-aged receptionist. "Morning, ma'am. I've got an appointment with Mr. Sanders at nine."

"Yes, Mr. Rainbolt. We're waiting for the other party."

"Other party?"

"Mr. Sanders will explain." She nodded toward the expensive-looking leather chairs.

"I'll stand, thanks." He cleared his throat. "The letter I received was fairly vague. Have any idea why I'm here?"

"I do. And Mr. Sanders will discuss the details with you soon." She offered a pleasant smile that revealed nothing. "Would you like a cup of coffee?"

"No, thank you." He paced back and forth a few times before he caught himself and stopped. Three hundred things on his to-do list at the ranch on a Monday morning, and here he was, all dressed up in a collared shirt and tie, waiting on a lawyer.

A moment later, the entrance door opened, and a woman took one step into the room. Her tote slipped to the polished oak floor with an echoing thud.

Reece reached for the leather bag, neatly scooping it up.

When he straightened, his gaze connected with the cool blue eyes of Claire Ballard. He did a double take as a roller coaster of emotions socked him in the gut.

Yep. Claire Ballard all right. There was no mistaking the proud tilt of her chin or the waves of chestnut hair that tumbled over her shoulders. She was more beautiful than he remembered. Time stood still as Reece offered Claire her bag. As if in slow motion, she accepted it and clutched the leather pouch to her chest.

She stared at him for a long moment, her face reflecting not only stunned surprise but something else he couldn't identify. Annoyance? Concern? Whatever it was, it was no doubt something he deserved.

He hadn't seen the woman in six years, and they hadn't parted on good terms. In truth, everyone who'd crossed his path six years ago probably came away praying to never run into him again.

Before Reece had the opportunity to pick his jaw up from the ground, the door of the attorney's office swung open and Edwin Sanders strode into the reception area. The silver-haired lawyer offered a benevolent smile as his gaze moved between Reece and Claire.

"Good to see you both," Sanders said with his slow-as-syrup Okie drawl. "Have you two met?"

"Yes." Claire said the word quickly without a glance in Reece's direction.

Confused, Reece looked from Sanders to Claire. She was the other party they were waiting for? What was going on?

Sanders turned to the receptionist as he ushered them into his private office. "I don't want to be disturbed."

Reece waited to be seated until Claire had settled in a wingback office chair, her legs demurely crossed and her hands clutched in the lap of her pencil skirt. She looked good, and he did his best not to keep verifying that fact when he eased into the chair next to hers.

The attorney sat and adjusted his suit coat before he opened a thick file on his desk. "I've asked you here today because Davis Ballard has made provisions for both of you in his will."

"My father's will? Both of us?" Claire's voice trembled and Reece blinked, his mind scrambling to be certain he'd heard the attorney correctly.

Sanders offered each of them a sheaf of papers. On the top was a topographical map of Ballard Farm that appeared to divide the property in two.

Ballard Farm consisted of one hundred and fifty acres of fruit and pecan trees and several greenhouses for fresh produce. Not only had Davis launched and managed the Rebel Farmers Market for as long as Reece could remember, but his farm also invited pick-your-own produce options to the public. A Rebel landmark, the orchard's pumpkin patch was the highlight of the fall season.

Why would Reece be mentioned in his neighbor's will? The question rolled through his mind as he assessed the papers in his hand.

"I don't understand, Mr. Sanders. When did my father change his will?" Claire asked.

"If you'll flip to the cover sheet beneath the map, you'll see that the will was amended only two months ago. April sixteenth."

Claire released a soft gasp. Her face paled and her lips became a taut line.

"Are you all right, Claire?" Reece asked.

"I'm fine." The words were a rote utterance that belied Claire's appearance as she stared past Sanders and out the window behind him. When she turned to Reece, he met her gaze and flinched at the raw pain in her blue eyes. Something about the attorney's answer had shaken her to the core.

Sanders stood and left the room, returning with two bottles of water, each moist with condensation. He handed one to Claire and the other to Reece.

Claire held hers to her forehead before removing the cap and taking a deep swallow.

"Do you want to continue?" the attorney asked. "We could reschedule. You've only recently buried your father. I know this is a difficult time."

"No. Please. Continue," she said. "I'm just tired. I drove here from Tulsa after working a night shift at the hospital."

Sanders nodded. "As you can see, Ballard

Farm has been divided in half per your father's request."

"Are you telling me that Reece inherited half of the farm?" Claire sputtered.

"That is correct."

What? Half the farm? He could honestly say he was as shocked as Claire was.

The ticking of the grandmother clock was the only sound in the room for a long moment as both Claire and Reece examined the map.

"According to this division, I have the family house on my side." She paused to study the map even closer. "It appears that the orchards are split right down the middle. That can't be right."

"Technically, the peach trees are on your side and the apple trees and pecans are on Reece's side," the attorney said.

Though Reece listened to the exchange carefully, the entire conversation left him with the unshakable feeling that he was missing an important piece of information. Information that might make sense of this meeting. Ballard Farm sat directly to the east of Rebel Ranch. Davis had been his neighbor, and he'd considered the man a friend. Close enough of a friend to leave Reece half his property? Probably not.

Why then?

Claire turned to Reece, her face a stormy mask

as she white-knuckled the paperwork. "Did you know about this?"

He raised his palms. "No, ma'am."

His answer seemed to agitate her even more. Great. He hadn't seen the woman in six years, and they'd parted on uneasy terms. Now here she was grieving and vulnerable and he'd managed to make things worse. All without even trying.

"I know this isn't what you expected," Sanders said to Claire. The words were gentle.

"No, it isn't. I'd planned to sell the property."

"Sell your inheritance?" The words shot out of Reece's mouth before he could lasso them back. He couldn't help his strong feelings about land and family. Selling Ballard Farm to strangers wasn't right.

Claire stiffened and she pushed her long hair away from her face. "There's nothing to prevent me from doing that. Am I correct, Mr. Sanders?"

"Yes. However, if you'll check page fourteen, you will note that Reece has inherited the water and mineral rights to Ballard Farm."

Reece cringed at the additional information.

"What?" Claire's single word was laced with a hint of desperation as she shuffled through the papers. "I have the land, but no water?"

"That is also correct."

"You're telling me Reece inherited the other

half of the orchard, the pond, the road, as well as the mineral and water rights?"

The attorney offered a solemn nod. "Your inheritance also includes the north barn, the utility building and the animals." Sanders slipped his glasses back on and assessed the paperwork. "One henhouse, two burros, and Blue." He frowned and looked up. "What's a Blue?"

"A dog," both Claire and Reece said at the same time.

Claire's face flushed pink, and she turned away from him.

A tense silence followed.

"Why would my father do this?" She massaged her forehead with her fingers. "I'm his only child."

"He was very specific about his wishes, Claire," Sanders said.

"And if I contest the will?"

"There are no solid grounds for contesting. Your father was of sound mind and in relatively good health and was not unduly influenced in his decision to amend the will."

"Relatively good health?" Claire's eyes rounded in alarm as she skirted to the edge of her seat.

"Aside from his longstanding cardiac condition."

She released a soft gasp. "What longstanding cardiac condition?"

"I may have overstepped here." Sanders flinched and shifted his gaze back to the paperwork. "I assumed you had privilege to your father's medical information since you're a nurse."

"He never said a thing."

"Claire, I'm sorry, but I don't have the authority to discuss that topic further. Perhaps his physician can give you more insight."

The room was silent as Sanders sorted through the paperwork. Reece allowed himself a glance at Claire, regretting that their friendship had deteriorated. He didn't have the right to take her hand and offer even a small gesture of comfort.

"If you'll turn to page sixteen," the attorney continued, "you will notice that your father provided a healthy trust fund for your daughter."

Reece blinked and jerked back his head at the words. Claire had a child? His attention moved immediately to her left hand.

No ring. He knew better than to make snap judgments or assessments. However, that didn't keep him from being confused. While Claire had proven successful at avoiding him for the last six years, the fact that Davis never mentioned a grandchild raised yet more questions. If Claire had a child, all the more reason the estate should go to her in its entirety.

"How is Zoe?" Edwin Sanders asked.

Claire's affect softened and a smile lit her mouth. "She's wonderful, sir."

"What happens if I don't want the inheritance?" Reece asked the question without preamble, causing Claire to turn and stare at him.

"If either of you declines the bequest, the entire inheritance reverts back to the estate, where it will be sold at auction. The proceeds will go to the City of Rebel."

"You must be kidding," Claire burst out.

"No, Claire, I'm very serious. You must accept the terms of the will as presented before you may entertain selling your share."

"You're saying Reece and I must claim our portion of Ballard Farm. Then we're free to sell?"

"Correct."

"That makes no sense. I can't sell if Reece owns valuable assets that affect my half of the property."

The attorney had no response to her legitimate assessment. But as Sanders reviewed the rest of the file, Reece remained silent. There wasn't anything he could say that would fix this situation he seemed to be knee-deep in. He didn't even understand all the dynamics going on today. What he needed was time alone with the attorney.

Another sixty minutes and half a dozen signatures later, the appointment was over. Sanders shook their hands and ushered them out of his office.

Reece held back, waiting for Claire to leave the building.

"You have a question, Mr. Rainbolt?"

"I sure do. Why did Davis leave me his land? We were neighborly, but that's as far as our relationship extended."

The attorney's face gave away nothing as he pondered the question for a moment. "I asked Davis the same thing. He told me you'd figure it out."

"Not exactly what I hoped to hear," Reece muttered.

No answers and plenty of questions. That's what the appointment had stirred up.

Hat in hand, he headed to the parking lot. Claire was only steps ahead of him, but her long legs moved like a filly being pursued. As if sensing his presence, she turned, opened her mouth and then shut it again. A phone began to ring, and she pulled a cell from her bag.

Reece hesitated. Should he wait? Clearly, he and Claire needed to talk, but he couldn't very well stand in the parking lot and eavesdrop.

"Everything is in the suitcase. Yes. I'm sorry. I should have gotten it out before I left this morning, but I was running late." Claire shook her head.

"I'll be at the farm shortly." She paused. "Are you sure? I can skip my errands if you need me."

A June breeze kicked up, ruffling her hair, and Reece once again tried not to stare. He'd known her all his life, but the majority of that time only in passing, because he and his siblings were from the south side of Rebel, and that made him not good enough for someone like Claire. Someone who lived in the big house at Ballard Farm.

Running into each other in Tulsa six years ago had been at a low point in both of their lives. It was collective grief that made them unlikely allies. He'd lost his little brother, Levi, at the same time that Claire was mourning the passing of the mother she'd only just reconnected with. Reece had walked away from his short-term relationship with Claire before she came to her senses and realized she was slumming. Yeah, he had made the first move before his heart had a chance to argue with his brain. Claire was a heartache in the making. No way would she settle for a broken rodeo cowboy with dreams bigger than his bank account.

Reece had been in a very bad place back then. It was Mitch who yanked him from the edge of self-destruction. Mitch, Rebel Ranch and God.

His head and his spirit might be in a better place now, but really, not much had changed. It didn't matter what his bank account now boasted.

He was still the kid from the wrong side of town with a questionable heritage, who never even went to college. When he looked at Claire Ballard, that hit home only too well.

Reece slowly walked to his truck. He'd find another time to talk to Claire—after all, she was right next door. At least for now.

For a moment, he sat in his vehicle and reviewed Davis Ballard's will, trying to make sense of his sudden inheritance. Though absolutely nothing would be gained by the directive, there was no way around the fact that Ballard Farm had been split down the middle.

Both pieces of the farm fit together perfectly like a puzzle.

He could sell his share of the inheritance to Claire after the paperwork was finalized. Then she'd turn around and sell everything. Was Davis trying to prevent that? Or was something else behind the decision?

Reece's gut said to slow down. Davis had a reason for leaving the property to both of them. No one goes out of their way to write a new will unless they have a good reason.

Before Reece made a single decision, he intended to find out exactly what that reason was.

I'm not a long-term kind of guy and I have zero interest in a future...with anyone.

The words offered by Reece Rainbolt six years ago mocked Claire as she was seated at a window table at Arrowhead Diner. She stared out the window, fighting the shame of the past.

What a fool she'd been—in love with a man who crushed her heart beneath his boot heel and walked away.

For the last six years, she'd assured herself that Reece wasn't a concern. She'd dismissed him in the same manner that he had coldly dismissed her.

After two hours in the attorney's office, she realized the error of her ways.

Reece was a huge threat.

She had been taken off guard by all of it—her father's death, the will and Reece. Then in the middle of the meeting, she'd been knocked to her knees yet again.

It was the moment that Reece offered a smile and a half laugh at something Edwin Sanders had said. Reece's mouth had turned up with a quirky grin and his deep blue eyes sparkled with humor.

Just like Zoe's.

Reece looked exactly like his daughter. *The daughter he didn't know about.*

"Ma'am? May I take your order?"

Claire looked up at the smiling face of a teenage server with a perky ponytail who placed a glass of water on the table.

"We have fresh peach muffins on the menu, served with peach jam made from Ballard Farm peaches."

At the unexpected reference, Claire couldn't hide a faint smile. Her father's dream might not be hers, but she was proud of his hard work.

"Perhaps later," she replied. "May I have a black coffee, please?" She hadn't eaten since last night at the hospital, yet her appetite lagged.

"Yes, ma'am."

Minutes later, a steaming mug of fresh coffee sat in front of her and Claire toyed with the handle as she continued to struggle to make sense of the morning. Around her, people enjoyed their meal as though all was well with the world. Just another day. But it wasn't. Not for her.

Stress pressed in on all sides. Losing her father due to a medical condition he'd kept from her. Decisions to be made about the farm. And then there was her job. While she loved her new position as night-shift charge nurse of a medical-surgical unit, the added pressure and responsibility had only grown in the past six months.

She sighed and caught herself. It seemed all she did was sigh. A clear sign she was overwhelmed.

When the door of the diner swung open, it caught Claire's eye. In walked the man who'd stolen her inheritance and held the power to take her future. Reece's gaze spanned the room until he spotted her.

Throughout the hometown diner, women discreetly turned their heads to check him out, their gazes lingering. He seemed oblivious. His gaze was fixed on Claire.

There was a time she would have done anything to have Reece Rainbolt's undivided attention.

Those days were long gone.

Claire gave him a covert assessment as he crossed the room, greeting a few people. Yes, he was handsome. Almost too handsome. Nothing about that had changed, nor had the fact that Reece was also tall and lean with a powerful build. She averted her eyes and reminded herself that he was the same arrogant cowboy who had walked away from her without a spare glance over those wide shoulders.

Reece was now well respected, an integral part of the community and ran a thriving guest ranch, or so her father said. She'd always changed the subject when he'd espoused the virtues of his entrepreneurial neighbor. Apparently, she should have been paying closer attention.

A moment later, Reece stood next to her booth.

"You followed me?" she asked without looking up. Instead, she took a sip of coffee, and she feigned interest in a water stain on the table as she willed her heart rate to slow down.

"No. I stopped to pick up supplies at the feed store and saw you through the window."

Claire glanced around. "Did you want something?"

"Don't you think we should talk?"

She released a tired sigh. Yes, they had to talk, whether she liked it or not. But not under the curious gazes of the Rebel gossip mill.

"Claire?" he pressed.

"Yes. We should talk. Just not here," she murmured.

"I'll stop by the farm tomorrow."

"No." Claire offered an adamant shake of her head. Not the farm. For nearly five years, she'd managed to keep Zoe safe from what she was certain would be Reece's rejection. She didn't have a contingency plan for what might happen now that she was tied to Ballard Farm.

"Do you want to come to Rebel Ranch?" he asked.

"Yes. That would be better. Thank you."

He pulled out his phone and slid his finger across the screen. "Maybe I can move some things around."

Move things around? Reece was a busy man. The only thing on her agenda was blessed sleep after a graveyard shift.

"How about nine a.m.?" he asked.

"That's fine."

Reece cleared his throat. "Listen, Claire. I'm really sorry for your loss. Your father was my friend. I regret that I was out of town for the service."

Claire looked up to find dark blue eyes searching hers. The unexpected compassion in his voice and the concern in his gaze threw her off for a moment.

"Thank you," she said.

"Tomorrow, then? Nine a.m."

"Yes."

He pulled out his wallet and slid a business card across the table. "My number. In case you have to cancel."

"Thank you."

Reece offered a nod before he turned away. Once again, all eyes were on the tall cowboy as he left the diner.

Claire sat back against her chair, shaken by the encounter. This was a new and improved Reece and she wasn't sure why or if she should trust this version.

"Ma'am, do you need a refill?" the server asked.

"No, thank you. I'm good." She lifted the mug and took a drink, then pulled a five-dollar bill from her purse.

Once she'd picked up a few things at the drugstore, Claire began a slow stroll through downtown Rebel. The Piggly Wiggly was still on Main Street. Someone had turned the old movie theater across from the Rebel Community Church into a Jazzercise and dance studio. There was even a brand-new community center and library.

Rebel was a pretty little town, mere miles from both Rebel Lake and Keystone Lake down the road. Idyllic and peaceful in the tourist off-season, flowers hung from giant pots on the street corners creating a picture-postcard of springtime ambiance. Rebel was even nicer than she remembered. She'd missed this little town and its whimsical shops and slow pace.

Whenever she visited her father, she'd made a point never to go into town, in an effort to avoid Reece. Like a ticking clock, she suspected time was running out on her options.

Claire kept walking, passing Eagle Donuts. At the corner, she spied a new bakery and crossed Second Street for a closer look. Daisy's Pies & Baked Goods was spelled out in gold lettering against a navy-blue background. Huge pots of yellow daisies and white petunias flanked the entrance, and two wrought iron tables with chairs filled the space outside the store window. *Very cute*.

But it was the window display of pink cupcakes with spiraled mounds of frosting and multicolored sprinkles that caught Claire's eye.

Zoe's favorite color was pink. Unable to resist, she pulled open the glass door. Melodic chimes greeted her along with the smiling face of the woman behind the counter. Her strawberry blonde hair had been braided and hung over her shoulder and she wore a white canvas apron over a pale yellow T-shirt emblazoned with the shop's name.

A cheery welcoming committee, Claire admitted.

"Hi, there. I'm Daisy Rainbolt."

"Rainbolt?"

"Yes. I'm married to Mitch." She cocked her head. "Are you new in town?"

"No. Back for a visit."

"You look familiar. Have we met?"

"I don't think so." Claire assessed the woman in front of her. Yes, she did look familiar, as well. Perhaps at her father's memorial service. That day last month seemed a complete blur. She'd been in shock and grieving. Her father was a young sixty-nine when he collapsed and died. Sudden cardiac death, his death certificate stated.

And it was only two weeks after she and Zoe had visited the farm. In fact, they'd planned to return again the next weekend, except she and her father had argued and she'd canceled her plans in favor of a short time-out.

Pain clawed at Claire's chest and she pushed the thoughts away. Guilt wasn't going to change things.

Instead, she inched closer to the glass case, concentrating on the cheerful sprinkles that covered the cupcakes.

"Two pink cupcakes, please."

"Excellent choice."

Claire straightened and glanced around the shop, which was painted in soft yellow shades. "So you're married to Mitch. Is he still police chief?"

"No. He works at Rebel Ranch. With our large brood, we both needed flexible hours."

"How many kids do you have?"

"Seven," Daisy said. "It's sort of a modified *Yours, Mine and Ours* situation."

"That's a nice-sized family."

"It is." Surprise danced in Daisy's bright blue eyes. She cocked her head. "And you're the first person who didn't jaw-drop at that number."

Claire chuckled. "I was an only child, so I highly respect big families and I'm a bit jealous. My little family consists of myself and a five-year-old." She hesitated for a second, thinking. "Somehow I thought I'd have a houseful by now."

The redhead leaned across the counter. "I can

remember having the same thoughts. Then, two years ago, I went from being by myself in my lonely apartment to adopting my orphaned nieces and nephews, and getting married. We were recently blessed with twins. If that wasn't enough, I now run my dream business. Never underestimate the power of a God who knows the desires of your heart."

Claire stared wordlessly at Daisy. She wasn't even sure what the desires of her heart were anymore.

The soft fussing of a baby filled the bakery and Claire looked around. "Did you hear a baby?"

"Yes. My twins are sleeping in the office. I have a baby monitor under the counter."

"Oh, my. You are a busy lady. What will you do if they need you?

"Roscoe, my assistant, will be right back. He ran to the bank. I'm covering the front for him."

"Can I help with anything?" Claire asked.

"You are so sweet. But no worries. If I have to, I can put a closed sign on the door."

"Now I'm in awe of your multitasking skills," Claire said.

"Don't give me too much credit. Behind this counter, I'm like a duck peddling as fast as I can." She paused. "You know, I didn't catch your name."

"My apologies," Claire said. "I didn't introduce myself. I'm Claire Ballard. My family farm is next to Rebel Ranch."

"Ballard Farm." A stricken expression crossed Daisy's face and she clutched her hands together. "Oh, my. You're Mr. Ballard's daughter. I'm so sorry for your loss. I didn't make it to the service because the twins had colds."

"Perfectly understandable," Claire said.

Daisy grabbed a sheet of bakery tissue and reached for the cupcakes, placing them carefully in a white box.

"So, you knew my father?" Claire asked.

"Oh, yes. Mr. Ballard always had a smile on his face when he delivered fresh fruit. Everyone in town liked him."

Claire smiled at the words. Once again, she found comfort in the knowledge that her father and his produce had touched people in Rebel.

"Anything else?" Daisy slid the box across the counter.

"How about a peach pie?"

"Another favorite, if I do say so." She grinned and leaned closer. "You and I have excellent taste. We should get together for coffee."

"I'd like that," Claire said, her mood lighter now than it had been all morning.

Daisy's grin seemed contagious and Claire couldn't help smiling back. She'd like to be friends with this woman. That is, if she were staying in Rebel. An unexpected prick of regret stung Claire. Except she wasn't.

Twenty minutes later, Claire pulled into the private family drive to Ballard Farm. Zoe spotted her, jumped down from the porch and raced across the expansive emerald lawn, ducking beneath the branch of a maple tree, with her long dark braids flying. Claire's heart swelled at the sight.

Nan Turner, the wife of Ballard Farm's crop production manager, Asa Turner, sat on the front porch, watching. What would she do without Nan? When Claire's mother left, Nan had stepped in whenever she could to do all the things that her father couldn't. Or wouldn't. Ever devoted to the land, he had buried himself in work, leaving Claire alone most of the time.

It was only six years ago that Claire was able to track down her mother who was in hospice. That was when she finally uncovered the truth about her childhood. Marta Ballard had an addiction. Her father used that as leverage to gain complete custody. Claire didn't know who she was angrier with, her father or her mother. They'd both denied her a childhood with their tumultuous marriage and abandonment of their daughter. Her mother to her addiction and her father to the orchards.

It took the birth of Zoe for Claire to make peace with her life. Zoe and the Lord turned things around. She found solace in her newfound faith as she worked to release the bitterness of the past.

"Mommy! You're back." Five-year-old Zoe leaped into Claire's arms the moment she stepped out of the car. Claire swung her around and then set her on the ground with a kiss to her forehead.

She grabbed the box from the car and turned around. "I brought you a treat, sweetie."

When Zoe's dark blue eyes lit up, Claire was again struck with the disconcerting awareness of how much they were like Reece's. An unusual shade of deep blue. She nearly dropped the box as she stared at her daughter. How had she never noticed?

Because she didn't have a single picture of Reece and in six years her memory had faded.

"Pink cupcakes?" Zoe grinned. "Thank you. Thank you."

"You're welcome. Bring them in the house for me, please?"

"Yes, Mommy."

Claire collected a few small bags from the car and started up the drive as Nan walked down to meet her.

Nan seemed to never age. Her dark hair, highlighted with sparse streaks of gray, was cut in a bob that touched her chin. As usual, she wore jeans and a blouse paired with black rubber muck boots. A wide-brimmed straw hat hung down her back from laces tied around her neck.

The older woman smiled when Claire held out another pastry box. "Oh, what's this?"

"A pie for you and Asa," Claire said. "Peach. No doubt made with Ballard peaches."

"Thank you." Nan smiled. "So you went into Daisy's bakery?"

"I couldn't resist."

"Pies are her specialty. Try as I might, I haven't been able to master her way with pastry. That woman is gifted."

"Well, then save me a piece." Claire shifted the bags in her hands.

"How did it go?" the older woman asked.

"Daisy is lovely. We're going to have coffee soon."

"No. I meant the will."

"Oh, that." Claire frowned as a shadow fell over her thoughts. "Did you know my father had a cardiac condition?"

"I knew he was seeing a doctor in Tulsa. But he never really discussed any of his health issues with me or Asa."

"Is Asa around?"

Nan turned toward the orchards. "He's out in the field somewhere. They're spraying the pecans today."

Following Nan up the drive, Claire glanced

around at the activity she spied in the distance. Workers moved in and out of the orchards and greenhouses. Past the barn, a tractor lumbered down the dirt road toward the fields.

What was she going to do with a farm? And half of one at that. Growing up, she'd done her best to pretend she lived anywhere but on a farm, even when she was plunked down in the middle of it, picking fruit. There was no way to ignore the truth now. "Things look busy," Claire said.

"Disease and insect control for the pecans. We'll be getting ready for the fruit self-picking season to start very soon. We've also got produce ready in the greenhouse. The first farmers market starts Saturday."

We. Nan and Asa managed the place along with a dozen seasonal employees. *We* definitely did not include her.

Nan stopped at the pathway to the front porch. "You own the place now, Claire. What are your plans? Will you be hands-on like your daddy?"

Claire shook her head. "I don't know how to run the farm."

"You lived in those orchards. You know more than you think you do."

"I have a career, a life in Tulsa." She took a deep breath and searched for a way to explain the turn of events that had happened in Edwin Sanders's office. "Nan, there is a problem."

"A problem?"

"Yes. My father's will." She hesitated for a moment and then barreled forward. "The farm was split down the middle with half going to Reece Rainbolt."

Claire shook her head. Things were much more complicated than that, but she didn't have the courage to admit to Nan or Asa that she wanted to sell Ballard Farm. The last thing she wanted was to hurt them.

"Reece Rainbolt?"

"Odd, isn't it?" Claire asked.

Nan's brows knit together, and she seemed to hesitate as if choosing her words with care. "I don't know if you're aware of it, but now that he's settled down, Reece is doing an amazing job with Rebel Ranch. He's brought in more tourists with that ranch than anyone would have figured. And tourists are good for everyone's business." She paused, thinking. "Still…"

"Why would my father leave half the farm to Reece?" Claire nodded. "Yes. That's the million-dollar question."

Nan was silent.

"Were they close? My father and Reece?" Claire couldn't imagine that. She came home a few weekends a month and had seen no evidence of that sort of relationship. Still, her father's pattern was to keep everything locked inside. All her life he'd been closemouthed with a tight rein on his thoughts and emotions.

"As close as your daddy was with any of his neighbors," Nan replied.

"Why Reece?"

Nan opened her mouth and then closed it again.

"What?" Claire asked.

"Sit down, honey." Nan pointed to one of the crisp white Adirondack chairs on the porch.

"Uh-oh." Claire obeyed the ominous words, climbing the steps and easing onto a cushioned seat.

"There was a time, about six years ago, after you tracked down your mother and she passed. You and your father were on shaky ground…" Nan paused. "You hadn't visited in nearly a year." She cleared her throat.

"Go on."

"I went into Tulsa to be with my sister for her hip surgery. Your daddy asked me to check on you."

Claire cocked her head and looked into Nan's clear hazel eyes. "I don't remember that we connected."

"We didn't. But I did see you."

"You did?"

"Yes, you and Reece. You two were coming out of your apartment building and you looked… well, happy."

Heat raced up Claire's neck and burned her face. "Why didn't you say something, right then?"

"I didn't want to intrude."

"And my father?"

"I mentioned it to Davis and he told me not to say anything. He was glad you were all right and that you found someone. I think he was relieved it was someone from Rebel."

Claire nearly choked on the irony. Found someone? Yes, someone from Rebel who broke her heart. Though, she'd never ever admit that.

"If he knew about Reece…" Claire paused and asked the awkward question "…why didn't he ever say something?"

Nan grimaced. "You know your daddy wasn't big on talk. And I think he was afraid he'd lose you again if he interfered."

Silence stretched between them. Claire fought off the demons of shame. She'd made some serious mistakes in the past. But that's exactly what it was. The past. She had committed her life to the Lord since then.

"You're going to have to tell him, you know." Nan said the words softly. She reached across from her seat to touch Claire's hand.

"Who?" Claire asked. Her thoughts still faraway.

"Reece. He needs to know he's Zoe's daddy."

Claire gasped and swallowed hard. "How do you know that Reece is…?"

"Honey, anyone with half an eyeball can see that little girl is the spittin' image of Reece."

"My father?"

"Farmers are notorious for knowing how to do the math."

In a rush, thoughts began to tumble into order in her mind. The last time she saw her father. He kept pushing her about Zoe's birth father. He'd stood by her without condemnation when she'd come home to Ballard and told him she was pregnant. And in all this time, he'd never pressed her for information. Until that last weekend.

It was as though he knew his days were numbered and he was getting his life in order and trying to fix hers. April 16, he had changed his will. Mere days after they'd argued.

If only they'd talked it out. Instead, the Ballards did what they do best. They went to their own corners and became silent and stubborn.

"Are you okay, Claire?"

Claire turned to Nan, terrified of what she'd see in the older woman's eyes. "Nan, Reece didn't want to know anything six years ago."

Nan smiled gently. "He's changed. So have you."

Fear began to stake a choke hold on her heart. Claire bit back emotion. "What if he decides Zoe needs to stay in Rebel?" She swallowed past the thickness clogging her throat. "What if he wants to take her away from me?"

"Now you're overreacting and getting yourself all worked up for no good reason."

"What about the fact that Reece owns half of this farm? What am I going to do about that?" Claire stood and paced back and forth. Reece wasn't a dirt-poor cowboy anymore. No, he was a prosperous and respected businessman.

"There's nothing to do about it right now," Nan said. "Just take it one step at a time, and try to remember that with a little prayer, things always have a way of working out."

Though Claire admired Nan's assurance, she admittedly felt anything but confident. At this moment, she didn't see any possible way for God to fix the mess she was in.

Claire made another pass across the porch and stopped when the screen door creaked open.

"Mommy, may I have a cupcake now?" Zoe called from the doorway.

"Sure, sweetie. Go ahead. I'll be right there."

"Are you off tomorrow?" Nan asked when Zoe disappeared.

"Yes. I had plenty of personal days accumulated, so I took two weeks."

"Good, because you look like you need a vacation."

"Do I?" Claire turned to examine her reflection in the tall windows of the porch. She pushed her hair back from her face. All she saw was the usual—dark shadows that reflected too many night shifts and too little sleep.

"You're wound tight as can be," Nan said. "And your eyes are filled with worry."

Claire didn't respond. Nan was right. Maybe a little rest and relaxation were in order.

Nan stood. "Two weeks is plenty of time to figure things out."

Plenty of time? Claire moved to the door and held the screen for Nan.

But was it enough time to persuade Reece to buy her out and make him understand why she'd never told him he had a daughter?

Chapter Two

"Any particular reason why you're checking your phone every five minutes?" Mitch asked. He turned from the white fence they were painting and eyed Reece.

"Am I?" Reece resisted the urge to pull his phone out again.

"Yeah."

"Claire Ballard is coming by at nine." *And he fully expected her to cancel.*

"Claire Ballard? Saw her at the memorial service. She sure has changed. I remember when she'd tag along with her father when he delivered fruit in town." He rubbed his chin with a hand. "Did you date her in high school? Or maybe I'm mixing her up with someone else. Then again, you dated every cute gal at Rebel High."

"Not Claire. She was a freshman when I was a senior. Claire volunteered in the school library in high school and she didn't date in school as I recall." And he did recall. He'd often find himself in the library watching her shelve books as he struggled over homework assignments. She was always polite when he had questions about locating resource books. Claire was one of the few people at Rebel High who saw him as a person, not just a pretty face or a dumb jock. That was enough to fuel a crush on her that he never told anyone about.

"The class bookworm, huh?" Mitch asked.

"Yeah," Reece said. "Funny how those labels seemed to matter back then, right?"

"Sure it mattered. Kids can be cruel. Our family was dirt-poor, which didn't help. The Rainbolt kids were always on the outside looking in."

"Yeah, but you know, bro, you made it all right for us. Like it was totally normal to be an orphan raised by my big brother." Reece assessed Mitch. The eldest Rainbolt had softened around the edges since he married Daisy, yet he remained the family rock. "At the risk of sounding sappy, thanks."

Mitch shrugged.

"Talking about those days always reminds me how fortunate I am to have you for a brother. You saved me after Levi died," Reece continued. "You were hurting, but you tucked it inside to yank me out of the path of my own self-destructive anger."

"It was more the good Lord than it was me. Most of the time I didn't know what I was doing. Functioning on prayers only."

"Yeah and you taught me to do the same. So again. Thanks."

"Yep, you're right. You're getting sappy. Knock it off."

Reece grinned and touched up a spot he had missed on the lower rung of the fence.

"So is she the reason you insisted the fence along the drive had to be painted ASAP?"

"What? Huh?" Reece looked up at Mitch. "No," he sputtered. "Been on my to-do list for a while. The fence is the first thing visitors see when they head up the drive. It's all about appearances."

"Right. All about appearances." Mitch paused. "Did you mention why Claire is coming to the ranch?"

"Long story," Reece mumbled.

Mitch glanced around before he dipped his paint in the can again. "Does it look like I'm going anywhere?"

Silence stretched with only the sound of wet brushes slapping against wood.

"Does this have anything to do with your appointment at Ed Sanders's office?" his brother prodded.

"How'd you know about that?"

"I went looking for you and found a letter from Sanders on the floor of your office. It was there for all the world to see." He snickered. "In fact, there were quite a few papers on the floor."

"That cat." Reece groaned. "Always walking across my desk. Knocking everything to the floor is her favorite pastime." He shook his head. "I blame Tucker. And myself. I should have said no when he asked me to take that calico in."

Mitch laughed. "I guess the advantage of being a younger brother and a vet is you learn how to manipulate your big brothers."

"Tucker has that move nailed." Reece stood back and observed his paint job. "Looking good."

"I'm sure that church group coming in at noon will appreciate our hard work."

"Church group?" He paused and searched his mental schedule. "You're right. I nearly forgot."

"That's not like you." Mitch narrowed his eyes.

"Have a lot on my mind lately," Reece said. A lot on his mind the last twenty-four hours was more like it. Ever since Claire walked back into his life.

"No worries. I'm happy to do the grand tour and get them settled."

"Thanks. You know, you're proving to be one of my best employees."

"I'd be your best employee if you'd loosen the reins and let me take more off your plate." Mitch pushed his Stetson to the back of his head with a finger and eyeballed him.

"You don't miss the Rebel police department?" Reece asked.

"Nice try. Changing the subject won't get you off the hook. But for the record, the only thing I miss is having Rebel's own Eagle Donuts personally delivered every Monday."

"Hey, boss."

Both Mitch and Reece turned at the words. Ranch hand Willard Cornell approached from the direction of the barn like a man on a mission. His John Wayne swaggering gait made him recognizable from a mile away.

Reece grinned at the sight. The old cowboy was so bowlegged you could run a herd of sheepdogs between his legs and he'd never notice. Willard kicked up dust as his boots moved him across the yard.

"Which boss do you suppose he's talking to?" Reece asked.

"It's you if it's bad news," Mitch said.

"I jest took a call on the barn landline. It was Violet at the front desk. She got a report that Baby is in the road."

"Again?" Mitch said. "That is the most stubborn cow."

"Why didn't V call me?" Reece asked.

"Said she tried," Willard replied.

Reece put down his paint brush and pulled out his phone. "Sound was off." He quickly scrolled through the screen.

"Ah, Reece."

"Yeah?"

"Your guest is here." His brother nodded toward the circular drive in front of the Rebel Ranch main house, where the ranch offices were located. A white Nissan pickup with the Ballard Farm logo had pulled up.

Reece startled at the sight, dropping his phone. When he reached for it, he bumped into Mitch's paint brush, getting a blob of paint on his black Rebel Ranch logo T-shirt.

"Careful," Mitch said.

"Now you tell me." Reece grimaced and grabbed a rag from the ground. "Great. Just great."

"She the new boss at Ballard Farm?" Willard asked.

"You could say that," Reece said. His gaze followed Willard's. Dressed in a flowered dress and sandals, her long hair tumbled past her shoulders as Claire walked around the truck. With oversized sunglasses perched on her face, she could be mistaken for some sort of celebrity. He continued to stare, unable to look away.

"Real pretty," Willard added. The old cowboy

pulled off his battered hat, slapped it on his thigh and covered his gray head again.

"Are you still here?" Reece asked.

"Yeah, I am. What do you want to do about Baby? Someone has to fetch her and it ain't gonna be me. That cow runs when I get within spittin' distance."

"That's because she overheard you bad-mouthing her. Baby is very sensitive," Mitch said.

"So you'll grab her?" Reece asked his brother.

"Sure I will. I'm partial to females with big eyes and long eyelashes."

Willard snorted at the comment.

"Thanks, Mitch." Reece turned to Willard. "Since you're hanging around, this fence is all yours."

"You told me to pick up the supplies in town," the old cowboy protested.

"Paint the fence and then go to the store," Reece said. "I have faith in your multitasking abilities."

"Fine," Willard grumbled.

When Reece turned his head, Claire spotted him and offered a nod of acknowledgment. He passed a hand over his face as he strode across the gravel. "Claire. Welcome to Rebel Ranch."

"Thank you." She paused, a bemused smile touching her mouth. "Um, you've got paint on your chin."

Reece pulled out a bandanna and swiped at his face. Of course he did. There went his plans to impress the woman. "Better?"

Claire nodded and glanced away. "Sorry, I'm late. There was a cow in the road."

"Yeah. My brother has gone to take care of the situation."

"That was your cow? I didn't know you ran cattle here."

"A dozen head for the guests. But Baby isn't part of the herd. She's a dairy cow. A rescue, courtesy of Rebel Vet and Rescue."

"You take in rescue animals?"

"Are you kidding? We're in danger of becoming the Rebel Animal Sanctuary if I'm not careful. My younger brother is a vet and we're his first stop. Last year we ended up with a goat as well as Baby." Reece shook his head. "Sometimes this place is like a three-ring circus. Today is one of those days."

At his words, Claire offered him a real smile, one that reached her eyes, and Reece was nearly knocked off his feet by the effect. He found himself as tongue-tied as a kid for a few moments.

"Sometimes a three-ring circus isn't such a bad thing," she murmured while looking around.

His gaze followed hers as she did a slow assessment of the property, her focus out toward the barn, the stables and the corral. "This land was pasture fields when I was growing up. You've really transformed things."

"I told you that was my plan," Reece said softly. He recalled sharing what seemed to be a pipe dream for the ranch six years ago with Claire. At the time, all he'd had were dreams and empty pockets after a short-lived rodeo career.

"Yes. You did…" Her voice trailed off as if she, too, remembered those conversations. Claire's face pinked, and she adjusted her tote bag under her arm.

The awkwardness between them could have filled a barn.

"How about we head inside to our offices?" He gestured toward the sprawling two-story white clapboard ranch house. "We can chat privately in the conference room."

"Oh, I thought this was *your* home."

"My house is up the road. This house was built on the foundation of my grandparents' home. Now we use it for reception, business offices and conference rooms. There's also a community area and the second floor has a few VIP suites."

"Impressive."

"Is it?" Was she impressed by what he'd accomplished since the last time they'd seen each other? He couldn't deny that a part of him hoped so. More than he'd like to admit. Maybe deep down inside he'd been waiting for this day. The day he'd be able to show her he'd made something of himself. He'd proved to the people of Rebel that Reece Rainbolt wasn't just a poor kid from the trailer park.

The prideful part of him needed to show Claire that while he'd never be in her league, he had done exactly what he told her he would do years ago. At the very least, his word meant something.

She followed him up the steps to a wide wraparound porch that boasted a row of rocking chairs for guests. Reece held the door and directed her past the reception desk where Violet Boerner waved to him. The pretty forty-something mother of five maintained her composure while juggling ringing phones and offering them a big smile.

"Busy place," Claire said.

"It is and now you've reminded me I promised Violet I'd hire her an assistant for the summer. Tourist season hits right after Memorial Day and that means we're swamped until Labor Day."

He led Claire past a billiards table and a giant flat-screen television surrounded by leather couches and down a carpeted hallway to a conference room.

"Something to drink?" Reece asked as he offered Claire a chair at the huge table.

"No, thank you." She sat ramrod straight in the chair and seemed to be steeling herself for their conversation.

Reece sat at the head of the table, giving her space. Though he tried to relax, it wasn't happening. He hadn't slept much last night, thinking about meeting with Claire today. It wasn't simply her opinion of him that mattered, though it did. Much more than it should. But it was the past. Six years was too long to go without righting his wrongs.

"I'd like to clear the air," he began.

"Clear the air?" Claire swallowed nervously. Her eyes shifted to the door as if contemplating a fast exit.

"I want to apologize for my behavior in Tulsa."

Claire opened her mouth, then closed it as if scrambling for an answer. Then her eyes became shuttered as the walls went up. Finally, she met his gaze, her eyes guarded.

"What exactly is it you're apologizing for?" she asked.

"Everything." Reece forced himself not to look away as he bit back shame. "I hurt a lot of people, including you, and I'm sorry."

"That was a long time ago." Her tone was icy as she continued. "We're adults and both of us have moved on."

"We were adults then, too, Claire."

She inhaled sharply and frowned, her blue eyes avoiding his. "I didn't come here to take a walk down memory lane."

"Fair enough." He paused, regrouping after the sting of her curt dismissal. "Why did you come here? To discuss how we're going to manage Ballard Farm together?"

Now she did look at him, her gaze direct. "I hoped you'd consider buying my share of Ballard Farm."

"What am I going to do with a farm?" The words slipped out rough and raw and he didn't even try to soften the delivery.

Claire stared at him for a moment in stunned surprise. Clearly, that was not the response she'd expected. "You could sell it once you have the entire property. Or let Asa Turner continue to manage things and extend your guest ranch," she finally said.

He searched her face for something, anything, to tell him what was really going on in her head. All he could find was a set chin and a determined expression. "Ballard Farm is your heritage. Doesn't that mean anything?"

She didn't answer.

"I guess not or you wouldn't have stayed away all this time."

Claire startled at the accusation, as fire banked in her eyes. "I didn't stay away. I was home to visit my father nearly every other Saturday."

Reece was silent at her words. This was news to him. Not once had he ever crossed paths with her in town. It was obvious now that she'd wanted to never run into him again and maybe he deserved that.

"You didn't answer my question." He narrowed his gaze. "Why are you so willing to give up your inheritance?"

Claire offered a slow, sad shake of her head. "You wouldn't understand."

"Try me."

A commotion in the hallway had both Claire and Reece turning their heads.

"No, Hazel. Stop. Ginger, wait."

"Tucker," Reece murmured.

"Your brother?"

"And his high-octane twins."

When Claire perked up, he realized that a surprise visit from Tucker and the twins might just salvage the disastrous meeting.

A redheaded brown-eyed child peeked into the conference room. Ginger. Then another face appeared. Fair-haired and blue-eyed Hazel. The girls were not identical, but definitely sisters. From their snub noses to their bow mouths.

"Uncle Reez!" they both cried.

Reece stood and scooped the four-year-olds up, one in each arm, as a moment later a harried Tucker raced into the room. Nothing softened his heart like his nieces and nephews.

"Sorry, Reece," Tucker said. "Didn't mean to

interrupt. Holding those two back is like trying to corral a greased pig."

Tucker nodded to Claire. "Ma'am. My apologies."

"Your daughters are adorable," Claire gushed.

"Tuck, this is Claire Ballard. Our neighbor."

"Ballard?" He paused, his face stricken with concern. "I'm so sorry for your loss, ma'am."

"Thank you," she said. "You knew my dad?"

"Your father visited the clinic often with Blue. Mostly he stopped by with donations for our rescue efforts."

"He did?"

"Yeah. Your father was a good man." Tucker cocked his head. "You used to work in the school library, didn't you?"

"All four years of high school. If it was a paying position, I'd be rich for all the time I spent there."

"I lived there a lot myself," Tucker said with a chuckle.

"Your name sounds familiar."

"I was a year behind you in school." He chuckled. "But I guess I've grown a few inches since then and I ditched the Clark Kent glasses."

"Tuck won't tell you, but he's the brains in the family. Earned a full-ride scholarship to Oklahoma State University."

"You went to OSU? Me, too," Claire said.

While the two shared college memories, Reece frowned at the strange irritation scratching at him. It only made sense that she and Tucker would have a lot in common. No way could he be jealous of his kid brother, whose path had been rougher than Reece's own with the loss of his wife. Yet, he couldn't help a wistful thought that it would be helpful if he and Claire had something to talk about besides Ballard Farm and their rocky past.

Reece cleared his throat.

"Sorry, didn't mean to hijack the conversation," Tucker said.

"Oh, it was just a quick business meeting," Claire corrected.

Right. It wasn't like they were friends or anything. When Tucker met his gaze and then quickly retrieved his daughters, Reece realized he'd been scowling like a cranky bull.

"I actually stopped by to be sure you were still on for babysitting tonight," Tucker said. "I've got that veterinary association meeting in Tulsa."

"I've got it on my calendar. I'm bringing dinner."

"Mac and cheese?" Little Ginger's eyes lit up.

"That's Uncle Mitch," Reece corrected. "I'm bringing my famous meat loaf and sweet potato casserole."

"Mmm," Hazel commented.

Reece turned to Claire and found her staring at

him with a mixture of what appeared to be surprise and curiosity.

"Thanks, bro," Tucker said. He offered Claire a nod. "Nice to see you again, ma'am."

"You, too." Claire stood and looked at her watch once Tucker left the room. "I have to be going. There's paperwork to fill out at the bank so the farm's employees get paid this month."

Reece didn't miss the small sigh before she continued. "I hope that by the time next month's payroll comes around, the situation with the farm has changed."

"How's that going to happen when we've hardly had a chance to discuss the will?"

"What else is there to discuss? Neither of us can run half a farm." She gave a dismayed shake of her head. "I've brought you a reasonable option. It makes sense to buy me out."

He could only stare at her for a moment. "Why did your father split the farm? Why leave half to me?"

"I don't know."

Yet, when he looked into Claire's eyes, there was something in the way she shifted her gaze that said she knew much more than she was willing to say.

"I'm going to have to give this some prayer," Reece returned.

Claire's eyes widened and the unsaid words hung between them.

"Yeah. I pray. Don't look so surprised. People change. Or maybe it's their priorities that change."

She stared at him for a long moment before she picked up her pouch. "Let me know what you decide. I've got a life in Tulsa to get back to."

"When?"

"When what?"

"When are you going back?"

"I've taken two weeks off."

He nodded. There were a lot of words he'd like to say right now, but he held back. The situation needed patience. Less talking and more praying.

They were both silent as he walked Claire to her car. He stood in the drive as the truck disappeared, all the while reviewing their conversation. Sure, he could buy her out and make her happy. A few signatures were all it would take.

That's exactly what a smart man would do. And after the mistakes of his past, Reece liked to think he was a smart man.

Except today, right now, his gut kept telling him to slow down. He couldn't help the dogged intuition that insisted there was more to the situation than met the eye.

Reece shook his head. He'd slow down, because if there was one thing he'd learned in the last six years, it was to listen to that gut feeling when it nudged him.

* * *

"The man is domestic and likes kids," Claire muttered. She added a dash of vanilla to the bowl of icing on the counter and fiercely beat the mixture.

"Did you say something?" Nan asked.

Claire's face warmed with embarrassment at the sound of Nan's voice. She turned to see her friend step into the kitchen. "Oh, I didn't realize you were back from town."

"Blue is quite the watchdog." Nan laughed. "He rolled over for a belly rub when I opened the door." She placed a paper grocery bag on the kitchen table. "I found those hair clips you needed and the Piggly Wiggly had butter on sale, so I grabbed you some, too."

"Thank you, so much."

"You were mumbling about Reece?"

"I guess I was." Claire pointed a spatula at the other woman. "Did you know that he's an accomplished cook and he babysits his nieces? It's the strangest thing." More than strange was the fact that since their meeting yesterday she kept having annoying daydreams of him in a little cottage with a picket fence and a wife and children.

Nan chuckled. "I think it's very attractive when a man isn't limited by antiquated gender expectations."

"Um…well, that's one way of looking at it."

The other would be that he'd been taken over by aliens. Much more likely, since the Reece she'd known years ago was vastly different from the man she'd met with yesterday at Rebel Ranch.

The old Reece had shown zero inclination for anything that resembled family life or business acumen. Quite the opposite. He had been estranged from his siblings, worked a variety of dead-end jobs and lived in a dismal low-rent furnished apartment in Tulsa. His culinary taste ran to pizza and junk food.

The fact that he'd seemingly changed so completely was confusing the well-structured wall of defense she'd built and all the reasons in her arsenal that validated staying clear of Reece. So what if he'd changed, Claire told herself. People said they'd changed all the time. Her mother insisted she'd changed and then picked up the bottle and walked out of her life, time and time again.

Change was a word. Nothing more.

Nan pulled a pound of butter out of the sack and put it in the refrigerator. "How was your meeting with Mr. Domestication?"

"Short and enlightening."

"I'm not sure if that's good or bad."

"Me, either." The oven beeped and Claire moved toward the sound. When she opened the door, the intoxicating aroma of cinnamon and orange teased her. Lightly browned and plump, the rolls clung together with moist swirls of cinnamon and butter, weaving a pattern between layers of dough.

"Oh, those look wonderful," Nan said.

"They do, don't they?" Claire smiled, pleased with her efforts. "I never would have thought to add orange zest to the cinnamon."

"Your mother's recipe, isn't it?"

"Is it my mother's? I was going through my father's paperwork and found a handwritten recipe tucked inside a folder." Claire paused. "I can't recall her ever making cinnamon rolls."

"Oh, my, yes. Your mother could certainly bake. Much better than me." Nan cocked her head. "You don't remember?"

"No. I wasn't much older than Zoe when she left and mostly I remember hiding under the covers with my hands on my ears while my parents had another round of arguments."

"Oh, my. I'm so sorry, Claire. But there were good times, lots of them, before she left."

Claire nodded, wanting to believe that was true. If it was, she had blocked it from her memories.

Nan's phone buzzed, and she pulled it out and read the screen. "That's another no." She released a small huff.

"Another no?"

"I'm recruiting volunteers to man the Ballard

Farm booth at the Rebel Farmers Market on Saturday. First one of the season."

"This Saturday?"

"Yes. I'd do it myself, but Asa and I are going into Tulsa. A birthday party for his mother. She'll be ninety-five."

"Wow. Good for her."

"I have a few more feelers out there, and I suppose I could always let Asa go to Tulsa by himself."

"No way." Claire grabbed the bowl of icing. "Don't do that. I can do the farmers market."

Nan stared at her. "Claire, your life has been turned upside down. The last thing I want to do is ask you to work on your vacation."

"Compared to the stress level of my job at the hospital, this sounds like fun."

"Are you sure?"

Claire looked up as it occurred to her that perhaps Nan didn't want her at the stand. It had been a very long time since she'd had her fingers in any of the farm's business. "You trust me, don't you?" she asked softly.

"Of course, I do." Nan put an arm around Claire's shoulders and hugged her. "Despite your protests, I know that you're a farm girl through and through."

The words shouldn't have made Claire smile. But they did. A part of her, deep down inside, was proud of the fact that she could handle many of the chores on the farm. She simply chose not to. "What are the hours?"

"It's only from eight until noon. The peaches won't be picked yet but we'll have plenty of produce from the greenhouses."

"Piece of cake. Zoe can help me," Claire said.

"You actually need a second booth mate. It can get quite busy. I'll find someone to assist."

"Okay, sure."

"I wasn't expecting such enthusiasm," Nan returned.

"Me, either." Claire shrugged. "You know, I always drove straight to the house when I visited Dad and avoided downtown Rebel. But I've been reminded what a nice little town it is. Maybe it will be good for Zoe to see that. It's her heritage."

"I couldn't agree more. Which is why it only seems natural for you to take over the farm. That's your heritage, too."

Claire was silent for a moment. How could she make anyone understand that, pray as she might, she couldn't get past the bitterness she harbored over what had been stolen from her and somehow it all seemed wrapped up in the land?

The only thing she could control was the future she gave Zoe. She wasn't going to allow her to be cheated of anything. Her daughter would get to be a child instead of growing up as a referee between two angry adults. Zoe wouldn't play second fiddle to Ballard Farm, either.

"I can't do it, Nan. Even if I wanted to. Which I don't. The truth is I can't afford to buy Reece out. I've looked at the numbers. The farm has been breaking even with a very modest profit. One late frost could mean the end of Ballard Farm."

Nan sighed. "Such is the plight of the small farmer."

"My only hope is to convince Reece to buy my half. Ballard Farm needs new energy and more money poured into it. Reece did that with his grandfather's ranch." She paused and cocked her head. "How do you suppose he did that, anyhow? Six years ago he was a broke-down cowboy with empty pockets."

"Not that I listen to the rumor mill," Nan said. "But I did hear that the Rainbolt kids came together after Levi died and they sold his portion of the ranch—the grazing land, northwest of the property. They used that as startup capital to finance the guest ranch business."

"That was a very smart move," Claire murmured.

"It was. Reece is a very smart man." Nan sank down into a kitchen chair.

"Which is why I think he's a good choice for Ballard Farm."

"What will it mean for the staff here? I mean, if you do sell to Reece. Will we all lose our jobs?"

"Why would he let you go?" Claire shook her head. "You and Asa wrote the Ballard Farm playbook and he certainly can't manage both businesses on his own."

"Honey, we aren't getting any younger. Asa and I are at that awkward age. Too young to retire and too old to find a new career path."

"Oh, Nan," Claire said. "I didn't even consider that someone wouldn't want you two to manage things. But unfortunately, I haven't persuaded him to buy me out yet. This is all speculation."

"You've got less than two weeks of vacation. What happens if he doesn't agree? What will happen to the farm?"

What *would* happen? A very good question. Her father had put her in an impossible position. Things were further complicated by the fact that harvest was upon them and Ballard Farm had two owners who weren't stepping up to take charge.

"I don't know what I'll do," Claire admitted. Worry had taken over her nights. She refused to let it steal her days, too. Instead, she concentrated on drizzling neat rows of icing on the warm pastry.

"Maybe you should bring him cinnamon rolls."

"Bribe Reece?" Claire laughed aloud. Judging

by his reaction today, it was going to take a lot more than cinnamon rolls.

"Couldn't hurt." Nan cocked her head. "I think all you two need is a little bit of time together to sort things out."

Claire was silent. The last thing she wanted was more time around Reece Rainbolt. Though in all honesty, she'd agree to almost anything if Reece would consider her offer and she could go back to the life she'd built for Zoe and herself in Tulsa.

"Mommy, Blue wants out."

"Coming." Claire peeked her head into the screened-in back porch. Zoe sat playing with her dolls while Blue scratched at the door to the yard. The yellow Labrador retriever whined when he saw her.

"I want to come, too," Zoe said.

"Put on your sneakers quickly, then."

Claire grabbed the leash and hooked it on the collar, then patted the dog's slick topcoat. "Good boy. You're going to behave, right?" Blue was high-energy and enthusiastic about his outings. Often too enthusiastic. He was nine years old but wasn't having any of that mature animal stuff. Her father never used a leash, but Claire didn't have the same results with her commands as her father. Blue pretty much laughed at her.

The threesome strolled briskly up the driveway along the green grass toward the Ballard Farm drive that led to the orchards, barns and the greenhouses.

The early June weather was comfortable, with the temperature in the low eighties accompanied by the typical Oklahoma humidity that Claire had grown up with. The difference here in the country was the delightful scent of ripe peaches that hung in the air. Overhead, the morning cloud cover had burned off, and the sky was clear and bright blue.

"Look, Mommy. A squirrel."

"Uh-oh."

Claire tried changing directions, but Blue noticed the squirrel and began to tug on the leash. She'd been through this before over the years. Blue had a low tolerance for ignoring squirrels and became fixated immediately. Claire pulled a treat out of her pocket to distract him.

"Here, boy," she cooed, offering squeaky kisses.

The lab tugged the leash as though Claire hadn't spoken.

"How come he isn't listening to you, Mommy?" Zoe asked.

"Because he didn't do very well in obedience school," Claire said.

Zoe laughed at her response.

"No, Blue." Claire firmly held the leash when the Lab surged once again.

"Blue wants that squirrel," Zoe said.

Her daughter was correct, and it didn't help when the mud-brown furry rodent wriggled his nose and dashed up the nearest tree, only to jump from branch to branch.

Claire and Zoe followed Blue, their pace quickening.

"Careful, Zoe. The ground is bumpy here." They crossed over the grass to the gravel of the orchard drive while Claire worked to hold Blue back. The feisty dog whined as the squirrel further taunted him by scrambling down the tree and circling the base, before running to the next tree in a wild game of hide-and-seek.

"Blue, heel."

"He's not heeling, Mommy."

"No, he's not."

When the Lab gave a hard tug, Claire lost the leash, tripped and flew forward into the dirt that circled the trees. "Oomph." She lifted her head and spit out a mouthful of red Oklahoma clay.

"Mommy, are you okay?"

"I'm fine. Just a little dirt." A little dirt, along with the reality that her thirty-three-year-old body didn't handle being slammed against the ground as well as it used to. She'd be sore tomorrow.

"That had to hurt."

Claire held very still. *No. It couldn't be. Not Reece.* When she moved to her knees and dusted herself off, Reece's hand appeared in front of her. Claire finally looked up and met the dark blue eyes. To his credit, there wasn't even a hint of amusement on his face, only what seemed to be genuine concern. She found herself caught in his gaze, unable to find a single word to respond as her heart tripped over itself.

"Let me help you up." He caught both of her hands and hauled her to her feet.

The quick move had her nearly stumbling into him. She was close enough to catch the heady scent of leather and man. Claire put a hand on his arm to steady herself. "Sorry," she murmured as she stepped back from his warm touch.

"Here." Reece dangled a navy bandanna in front of her.

"Thank you." Claire took the offering. She wiped the dirt and hot humiliation from her face before meeting his gaze again. He looked like an outlaw, dressed in a black Rebel Ranch logo T-shirt with his blue jeans. His dark brown hair peeked out from beneath a black cowboy hat. She couldn't help but notice his silver trophy buckle—a reminder that he was still a rodeo cowboy at heart.

"Where did you come from?" she asked.

He inclined his head behind him. "Other side of the fence."

Claire assessed the five-foot split rail fence that

separated their properties. On the other side, a black stallion grazed beneath a redbud tree.

"You jumped over that fence?"

"I guess I did." He grinned, revealing straight, even teeth and a dimple she'd forgotten about. "To tell you the truth, I didn't know I could still move that fast."

A bubble of laughter slipped through Claire's lips. She couldn't help it. The entire situation seemed comical.

"You're in an awfully good mood for someone who just face-planted," Reece said.

"What can I say? I've got two full nights of sleep under my belt."

"Sure. I get that."

Beside her, Zoe tugged Claire's hand. "Mommy, where's Blue?"

"I'll find him and bring him up to the house," Reece said.

"Oh, I couldn't ask you to do that," Claire said.

"Not a problem. I used to fetch him for your father all the time. Chances are Blue is over the fence playing in our pond by now."

"Seriously? My father said your pond is well past the orchard."

Reece smiled. "Those Labs love the water."

"I'm more than appreciative, then. Thank you."

"This must be your daughter?" Reece frowned as his gaze assessed Zoe.

Claire tensed. This was the moment she'd played over and over in her head. The moment Zoe met her father. In her carefully orchestrated daydreams, she somehow imagined she'd be in control of the situation.

"Zoe, this is Mr. Reece."

Her daughter peeked out from behind Claire. She pushed a strand of hair from her eyes and stared at Reece, her dark blue eyes curious.

"Can you say hello?" Claire prompted.

"Hello."

"Hi, there." He knelt and offered Zoe a smile. "I'm thinking you're the same age as one of my nephews."

"I'm five," Zoe said proudly.

"Five, huh? Almost ready to start school."

"Uh-huh," Zoe said with a proud nod of her head.

Reece blinked as if processing the information. He stood and looked at Claire long and hard before he turned to Zoe again. A chill passed over Claire as she realized he was doing the math.

Oh, Lord. Not now, not here in front of Zoe. Please.

"If you want to come up to the back porch, the screen door is open," Claire said. The words were a tumbled rush from her lips.

"Yeah. Yeah. I'll do that." Reece offered a distracted nod and headed down the fence line.

"Who's that man, Mommy?" Zoe asked.

"Mr. Reece is our neighbor. And he's a friend of your grandpa's."

"My grandpa in heaven."

"Yes."

"Will Mr. Reece find Blue?"

"Oh, I imagine he will."

Reece would find Blue because he was good with animals like her father. And it was likely that he was good at math, too.

Claire swallowed hard before she released a long breath. No matter how many times she'd played out the scenario of facing Reece and delivering the truth, nothing could have prepared her for today. Her stomach was in knots as she took Zoe's hand and started toward the house with the knowledge that her life had tilted upside down and things were about to change forever.

Chapter Three

"You found Blue!" Zoe's voice rang out.

Reece looked up at the greeting to find Nan Turner and Zoe walking toward him.

Zoe. She was a miniature Claire, with waves of dark hair and her mother's straight nose and finely arched brows. Except for her eyes. Zoe's eyes shook him to the core. There was no doubt in his mind that those dark blue eyes were the same ones he saw when he looked in the mirror.

His daughter.

An ache settled in his chest, making it almost difficult to breathe.

His child.

"Reece?" Nan asked. "Are you all right?"

"Yeah. Yeah. Sorry." He released a breath and scrubbed a hand over his face.

"Did you hear me, Reece?"

"I guess not," he murmured.

Nan cocked her head, eyes questioning. "I asked where you found Blue."

"Blue? He was sitting in a mud puddle staring up through the branches of an oak. That ole boy treed a squirrel and was pleased with himself."

"So that's why he looks like he was dipped in chocolate," Nan said with a laugh.

The Lab seemed to enjoy the attention and looked back and forth at the humans with a breathy pant as his tail thumped with joy.

"Thank you for finding Blue, Mr. Reece," Zoe said.

"You're very welcome, young lady."

Zoe's round cheeks pinked at his words, and she giggled.

Reece couldn't help but smile again. Man, she was cute. Did Claire look like Zoe at that age?

Five years old. Try as he might, he couldn't wrap his head around the fact that he had a daughter. Thoughts raced through his mind like a dog chasing his tail.

Obviously, Zoe had no idea he was her father. What had Claire told her?

Nan looked between him and Zoe. "You two have met?"

"We have," Reece said.

"Mr. Reece, the chicken had babies," Zoe interjected. Her eyes shone with excitement. "We're going to see the baby chicks."

"You are?" he returned.

"Uh-huh." Zoe nodded and offered him a shy glance. "Do you want to come?"

"I do, but I need to talk to your momma," he said. "Maybe I can come next time."

"Okay," Zoe said softly.

"Why don't you let me take Blue with us?" Nan asked. "We can hose him off."

"What if he escapes again?" Reece asked.

"I'm sturdier than Claire. He won't escape. That dog knows I mean business." Nan's expression dared him to doubt her. "Hand that scoundrel over."

"Yes, ma'am." Reece offered Nan the leash. "I'd give him plenty of lead unless you want a mud shower."

Nan laughed. "Is that what happened to you?"

He looked down at himself and assessed the splatters of red soil decorating his clothes. "Yep. A Blue shake-off."

Nan started to go and then turned back. "You're going to talk to Claire?"

Reece blinked at the concern in her eyes. And then he realized.

Nan knew.

Did everyone know except him? What about Asa Turner and Davis Ballard? Question after question pummeled him.

"Reece? Are you sure you're okay?" she asked quietly this time.

He sucked in a ragged breath and struggled to calm himself. "I don't know what I am, to tell you the truth."

"I understand and I know this isn't easy," Nan said. "But try to be kind."

"Kind?"

"Yes. Be kind to one another, tenderhearted…"

"Ah. *Ephesians.* I'll keep that in mind." He stepped back and smiled at Zoe, as sadness washed over him. He'd missed so much.

"See you later, Mr. Reece." Zoe raised a hand and wiggled her fingers in a little wave as she skipped away.

The walk to the Ballard house seemed to take forever. Shame dogged Reece's steps.

Halfway there, mad began to sneak into his thoughts and he fought back against the emotion. Not going there. Not anymore. The Lord was in charge now, and he refused to let anger rule him again.

Reece kept walking.

The internal battle left him drained and confused by the time he climbed the steps to the Ballard house. Before he could knock, Claire appeared and held open the screen.

"What happened to you?" she asked.

"Blue shared his mud with me." Reece kicked

off his boots and left them outside. He stepped in the house, his gaze fixed anywhere but on her.

"I'm so sorry." Claire looked past him. "Where is he?"

"Nan took him. She said she'd hose him down."

"Thank you for all your trouble."

"May I wash up somewhere?" he asked.

"Yes. Yes. Of course. First door on the left." She directed him down the hall.

Reece washed his hands and forearms and splashed water on his face. Then he stared at himself in the mirror. All these years and he was still his father's son. He had vowed to never be like TJ Rainbolt, who'd abandoned him and his siblings. Yet, here he was, about to face the truth. He closed his eyes and dried his face.

"Forgive me, Lord," he whispered.

The sounds of an automatic coffee maker spitting into a glass carafe greeted him as he stood in the doorway of the spacious kitchen. It occurred to him that he'd never been inside the Ballard house. He wasn't a decorating expert but his first impression said that the decor was a bit dated. Like time stood still. That rang true with what Claire told him years ago—her mother left when she was in kindergarten. Though it needed a refresh, the place was a couple dozen pay grades nicer than the trailer he'd grown up in.

Claire placed two mugs on an oak kitchen table

and turned toward him just as he stepped into the room.

"We need to talk," he said.

"I agree. It would be good if we could come to an agreement about the farm before I go back to Tulsa." She nodded toward the kitchen table. "Have a seat."

He complied and slid into a chair.

"You take it black, right?" Claire picked up the coffee carafe and poised it over his mug.

"Yeah, right." Six years later and she remembered how he took his coffee, but she forgot to tell him he had a daughter. Reece bit back the hurt and prayed for patience.

"Cinnamon roll?"

"Huh?" He met her gaze.

"I made cinnamon rolls," she said.

"No, thank you." He cleared his throat. "Could you sit down?"

Wariness flashed in her eyes. "Yes. Sure."

Reece put his hands around the mug as Claire settled in a chair across from him. "I'm not here to talk about the farm." The words hung awkwardly between them as he struggled to continue. "Why didn't you tell me?" he asked, unable to hide the raw pain that accompanied his words.

"Tell you?" Claire grimaced and lowered her eyes.

"Don't pretend you don't understand the question. Zoe is my daughter. Why didn't you tell me?"

Claire's face paled. "It's not a simple question, Reece."

"Yeah. Right. Now you're going to tell me it's…complicated."

"You walked away and told me you wanted nothing to do with any sort of future with me. So, yes, things did get complicated when I found out I was going to have a baby."

He blinked and looked at her "You couldn't call me? Holler across the fence. We're neighbors."

"Why would I? You told me that you had no use for marriage and even less use for kids."

Reece swallowed. Yep, he'd said that. Every word.

Though he'd taken some tough hits in his life, this was truly one of the worst. Right up there with losing his mother and his brother. And he had to claim responsibility for most of this sucker punch.

He'd lost the opportunity to raise his own child. Claire was so certain he'd be a lousy example of a father that she hadn't even given him a chance to prove she was wrong. He almost didn't blame her. Almost.

"Both of our lives and Zoe's might have been different if you had called me. I would have done the right thing, Claire, and I'm sorry I wasn't there for you."

"It doesn't matter. Trust me, the last thing I needed was a marriage like my parents'."

Except it did matter. He knew it and she knew it. "Instead, you chose to raise our child alone."

"I knew I could do that. I'm an only child raised by a single parent. I'm used to being alone. I am used to people walking away from me and fending for myself." She paused, her breath hitching as a bleak, distant expression filled her eyes. "My daughter will never face that kind of rejection."

Heart hammering, Reece straightened as her words slugged him full-on. "You convicted me of a crime I didn't commit. I would have never rejected our child." He sucked in a breath of indignation. "We could have worked things out with a simple conversation. Normal people talk, Claire."

"Normal people? I have no frame of reference for what you seem to think is normal behavior."

"That's your excuse?"

"It's not an excuse." Her voice took a hard edge as she clutched her hands together on the table. "It's the truth. And every year that passed it became harder and harder to think about contacting you and being rejected again."

"Did Davis know? Is that the rationale behind the will?"

"I believe my father came to the conclusion that you're Zoe's father. But I never told him anything about you."

"Why not? Why didn't you tell him?"

"That's not the issue," she said without looking at him.

Reece chewed on that answer for moments. He shook his head. "All these years, I envied you."

"Me? Whatever for?"

"You lived in that big house and had all that land, and your father was Davis Ballard."

"I'm grateful for all my father provided for me. However, inside my glass house, things were very different."

The hum of the refrigerator roared in the silence for a long moment.

"What about Zoe?" Reece finally asked. "What did you tell her about her father? About me?"

"Zoe is five. She wants simple answers right now. That's what I give her."

"That doesn't make sense."

"It does to a five-year-old. She knows she has a father who loves her, who doesn't live with her."

"And who watches Zoe when you work?"

"I work graveyards and pay nursing students to sleep over. They study and then sleep on the couch."

"When do you sleep?"

"That's a very good question. Not often enough. When Zoe starts school in the fall, I'll switch to the day shift."

For the past five years, she had sacrificed her

sleep for their child. There was no doubt Claire was a good mother, a devoted parent. He deserved the same chance. Reece took a deep breath.

"I want to share parenting." The words were out of his mouth before he could have second thoughts. And then he realized there were no second thoughts about this situation. He wanted to be Zoe's father.

"Share? Share how?" Fear filled Claire's eyes as she stared at him. "I work in Tulsa. Are you talking about weekends?"

"I have time to make up for, Claire. I want more than weekends."

"But…but, she doesn't know you. You can't expect to simply step into her life without preamble."

"Switch to the day shift now and leave Zoe with me when you're working."

"You're a stranger."

"I'm her father." He looked at her.

"But you have a job, too."

"I'm the boss. My schedule is much more flexible. Besides, she has cousins here for playdates and family."

"Family." Claire murmured the word.

"What do you say?"

"I don't know." Claire leaned back in the chair, shoulders sagging.

"We can do this amicably or I can get a court order for a paternity test and file for custody."

Eyes moist, she raised a hand to her mouth. "You aren't being fair."

"Fair," Reece murmured. There were more questions standing between them than there were answers. He stared out the big kitchen window at the orchards in the distance. Peaches ready to harvest, and apples right behind. As his gaze focused on the slow-moving blades of an ancient windmill in the distance, an idea began to whisper inside. He turned to Claire once more.

"Look, Claire, the way I see it, you want something and I want something."

"Pardon me?"

"You want me to buy Ballard Farm. I think there's a solution that we both can live with."

"I'm not following you."

"I'll consider buying Ballard Farm if you consider a leave of absence so I can get to know my daughter."

Her eyes rounded. "A leave of absence? For how long?"

Reece stared at the calendar tacked to the wall. "I spoke to Asa earlier. The orchards are nearly ready for harvest."

"Yes. The peaches are. Followed by the apples from mid-August to October. The orchard harvest spans over five months. We don't even start to harvest the pecans until September." She paused. "And Zoe is registered for school in Tulsa right after Labor Day."

"Okay. Stay through August. Walk me through harvesting the fruit. And in our downtime, help me get to know my daughter."

"Reece, I have a career in Tulsa. One I have worked very hard for." She shook her head. "You're being unreasonable."

"Am I? All I'm asking for is a little time to get to know my daughter." He paused and met her gaze. "You've had five years."

Flustered, she seemed to search for a response. "But the farm… I don't know anything anymore."

"You know more than you think. You were raised here. Asa told me you worked the farm until you left."

"Oh, sure. Years ago."

"I guess we'll learn together."

"That's ridiculous," she sputtered. "How can you possibly have time to spend at Ballard when you're managing Rebel Ranch? You said this was your busiest season of the year."

That was a very good question. One he didn't plan to address until he'd spoken to Mitch. Until then, he'd sidestep.

"That's the deal, Claire. Three months working the farm and getting to know my daughter. Then I'll buy you out. I've already spoken to my attorney and he's working on a draft of an amicable custody agreement. Of course, I'll be providing you with compensation for back child support and expenses."

"A custody agreement?" Her face paled.

"A draft of something we can both agree upon is what I said."

"Right. Right." She released a breath. "In the meantime, I don't want your money, Reece."

"Then bank it for Zoe's future."

"So just like that, you're suddenly agreeing to buy the farm?"

"I won't be buying the farm. Rebel Ranch would be." He met her gaze. "You said that's what you want, and I think you're right. Ballard Farm should be handed down to Zoe and I'm going to do that."

Silence stretched between them.

"Surely you don't expect me to decide right now."

He pushed back his chair and stood. "I'll need an answer by Sunday."

Turning, Reece spotted a photograph of Zoe with her grandfather tacked on the refrigerator. He froze. Zoe. She was the reason Davis left him half of his farm.

A peace settled over him.

Davis had known Reece was Zoe's daddy. It was a mixed blessing, as Davis's too-soon passing had provided Reece with a second chance. A chance to be a father to his daughter. And a chance to somehow make Claire understand that Ballard Farm was their daughter's future.

Claire's stomach grumbled as tantalizing aromas from the farmers market converged. The yeast and buttery scents of fresh bread and sweet pastries, along with a waft of cinnamon from roasting pecans, made her regret skipping breakfast.

The Rebel Farmers Market was held in the parking lot of the Rebel Community Center, where most vendors hurried to complete setup as the 8:00 a.m. hour neared.

Directly across from her, the baby-blue-and-white-striped awning of the Eagle Donuts booth flapped gently in the morning breeze. Already open for business, Eagle had a line of customers eager for coffee and breakfast treats.

"Mommy, I smell something good," Zoe said.

"Me, too." Claire removed protective paper from a flat of melons and turned to her daughter. "As soon as I get this produce unpacked, we can go get a snack. Okay?"

Zoe nodded and returned to the coloring book in her lap.

Asa had delivered the Ballard Farm produce to Claire, along with a pricing sheet and a cash drawer before he and Nan headed to Tulsa. Claire was ready and eager. The farmers market provided a much-needed distraction from her current concerns.

She'd been walking around stunned and confused since her conversation with Reece on Wednesday, unable to believe that she was stuck on Ballard Farm for three months. Like a prisoner.

Somehow the tables had been turned on her. All she'd wanted was to sell the farm, and now she was part of some grand scheme Reece had for saving Ballard for Zoe.

The whole thing left her unsettled. Was he right? Had her childhood left her thinking so skewed she couldn't objectively see the situation? Ballard was her father's life, but did that make it hers and Zoe's, too?

It had been three days since Reece's ultimatum. Three days of scrambling to put her life on hold had left her tossing and turning every night.

Though her nursing supervisor was not pleased, Claire had submitted the paperwork to use up all of her vacation and sick leave and requested a leave of absence through the end of August. Unfortunately the paid time off would only last another few weeks. It wouldn't be long before she'd be without a paycheck, though the bills would continue to arrive.

One worry at a time. Soon she'd need to drive to Tulsa to pack what she and Zoe needed for the summer and take care of a handful of other matters, like her mail and the plants she'd nurtured in the kitchen window.

Another strong waft of food teased Claire and she groaned while tossing the last of the packing paper into a recycle box. Now she smelled coffee—fresh, hot and strong. Oh, why hadn't she brought a travel cup?

"Donuts anyone?"

At the sound of the male voice, Claire froze and then swung around. *Reece?* Yes, it was the man. Tall, lean and ridiculously handsome. Without his usual Stetson, he seemed almost boyish. And didn't it just figure that she'd wound her hair into a messy bun and donned old jeans and a faded green Ballard Farm polo shirt that predated college.

"Mr. Reece!"

"Hi there, Zoe." He paused for a moment and stared at her, his eyes filled with a wondrous curiosity.

"What's in the box, Mr. Reece?" Her daughter abandoned her coloring book and crayons and jumped up, leaning over the table to see Reece's offerings.

He flipped open the lid to reveal frosted pink cake donuts with sprinkles.

"My favorite. Pink and sprinkles."

"I took a chance. I thought you might like this kind." Then he froze. His gaze shot to Claire, a panicked expression on his face. "I guess I should have asked first. Tucker is always after me for that."

"It's fine," Claire said with a longing glance at the box. "We don't make a steady diet of sweets, but an occasional treat is nice. Besides, I was getting ready to go over to Eagle myself."

"Great. Here you go." He slid the baby blue box onto the table and handed her a carrier with two coffee cups.

She glanced at the tall cup of coffee, then met his gaze. "Thank you. I am very grateful."

"We've got to have sustenance for this job, right?"

We? Claire stared at him, as he moved around the table and into the booth. "You're working with me?"

"Is that a problem?" He took a coffee cup from the carrier and took a sip.

"Um… No, I guess not."

"Nan said she thought it might be good for us to have more time to talk."

Claire had a sudden flashback to her chat with Nan in the kitchen.

All you two need is a little bit of time together to sort things out.

And she clearly recalled thinking she'd do most anything to get Reece to consider buying Ballard Farm. Never in a million years did she think that would include spending the summer in Rebel and working side by side with her daughter's father.

She took a donut from the box and grabbed a coffee before she retreated to her half of the ten-by-ten booth. Her side.

Claire glanced down at Zoe, who sat on the folding chair right between them licking frosting off her fingers. Lifting her gaze, Claire saw Reece, too, was looking at Zoe with wonder in his eyes.

A sharp pain grabbed Claire's heart. *Have I made the right decision?* The question whispered through her mind, and she quickly chased it away. She did what she had to do.

"Good morning."

Both Claire and Reece looked up. Tucker approached the booth with a broad smile on his face as usual.

"Good morning," Claire returned.

Tucker turned to his brother. "You're working the Ballard booth?"

"I'm being neighborly," Reece said.

Tucker chuckled as though there were an inside joke going on. "I can see that."

"Don't you have somewhere to be? I thought you had an adoption event today," Reece grumbled.

"I'm headed there now." Tucker pointed to the other side of the expansive parking lot. "It's over there, by the grass, so we can give the puppies a little run time."

"Puppies?" Zoe's head popped up and her eyes rounded.

"Puppies *and* kittens," Tucker said.

"Tuck, this is Zoe. Claire's…um…"

"My daughter," Claire said.

"Yeah, right. What she said," Reece continued. "Zoe, this is Mr. Tucker. He's my little brother."

"Hi, Zoe." Tucker turned to Claire. "I'm happy to take her to see the animals. My girls are over there right now. Jena, the other vet, is watching them."

"Please, Mommy." Zoe clasped her hands together, as if in prayer. "Please."

"I… I…" Claire sputtered.

"I'll keep a close eye on her." Tucker lifted a hand in oath. "I'm a father and a vet. No outstanding warrants, not even an overdue library book."

Claire smiled. "You know how it is," she murmured.

"I do. I totally get it."

"She can go," Claire said. "Thank you."

Her daughter hooted with delight. "Oh, yes. Thank you. I love puppies, Mr. Tucker."

"We can't have puppies in our apartment, Zoe," Claire said.

"What about goats?" Tucker asked. "Goats are low-maintenance."

Claire gasped. "Goats?" She looked at Tucker. "Not really?"

Tucker started to laugh. "I'm kidding, Claire."

Reece shook his head. "Claire is very literal, Tuck."

Was she? Claire frowned at Reece's words. The man hadn't seen her in six years and literal was his takeaway. Apparently, she was as memorable as she suspected.

Her gaze followed the vet and her daughter as they weaved through the crowd to the other side of the parking lot.

"Hard for you to let her out of your sight, isn't it?" Reece asked.

"I'm not a helicopter mother." Or maybe she was. After all, it had been just her and Zoe for so long.

"What do you think about you and Zoe coming to the ranch? Maybe ride a horse. Both of you. You can keep a close eye on her."

"Isn't she a little young for horseback riding?"

"Not at all."

"I don't know." Claire hesitated.

"Let her at least come and see the horses? Let me show her around Rebel Ranch. The ranch is as much her heritage as Ballard Farm."

Claire paused at his words. Rebel Ranch was

Zoe's heritage. She hadn't considered that before now. It only added to the complications of the situation.

"You okay?" Reece asked.

"Yes," Claire murmured. She faced Reece. "Don't take this the wrong way, but I don't want you to pull the rug out from under Zoe."

"Excuse me?" He crossed his arms as though working hard at patience.

"Give her some time to get to know you. Then we can tell her that you're her father."

"Where do you suggest I start?" Annoyance laced his voice.

"How about if Zoe and I give you a tour of Ballard Farm? That's familiar to her and to me."

"Can't say that I understand what the difference is. Your place or mine. But I suppose it doesn't matter. All that matters is that I get to spend time with my daughter."

"What day works for you?" she asked.

"Friday's a slow day." He pulled an envelope from his back pocket. "Before I forget."

"What's this?" Claire took the plain envelope and turned it over.

"I contacted the ranch attorney in Tulsa. This is the back child support he recommends."

"What?"

"I know this in no way compensates you for the last five years…"

Claire huffed. "Are you trying to buy me off?"

"Not at all. In truth, this is more about me doing the right thing."

"The right thing. And what about custody? You said you were going to discuss that with your attorney, as well."

"I told him to put together something for us to look at down the road, that's all."

That's all. Maybe in his world that was all, but not to her. Words like custody were the things that kept her awake at night.

"Well, if it isn't young Reece Rainbolt."

Both Claire and Reece looked up. The man who sidled up to the booth wore a straw cowboy hat, which sat on the back of his headful of thick silver hair. "Ms. Ballard. I don't believe we've met officially." He stuck out a hand. "Bernard Hall. I saw you at the service. Apologies for not coming up to offer my condolences. My wife is homebound and I had to skedaddle back to the house."

"It's very nice to meet you, sir."

"Nice selection you have here." Bernard nodded as he inspected the fruit, his attention lingering on the melons. "Ballard Farm always has the best produce."

"Thank you," Claire said.

"What kind of cantaloupe are these?"

"Ambrosia," Claire said. "They're a hybrid that produce a sweeter, juicier melon."

He picked one up, examined the melon closely and then set it down again. "You sure this is ready?"

"Yes, sir, see that yellowish-gray color between the netting? That's the indication of a melon ready for your plate." She lifted it up and sniffed, inhaling the sweet and pleasant aroma. "Oh, yes. I'd say this is perfect."

"I'll take it." He slid a bill across the table.

Claire reached for a paper bag at the same time as Reece. When their fingers collided, she nearly jumped back.

"Sorry," he mumbled.

"Why don't I let you bag the melon," she said. "I'll get Mr. Hall his change."

"Thank you, ma'am," Bernard said as he pocketed his coins. "And glad to see you stepping into your daddy's shoes. People come and go in this town, but the land—it's something to pass down to your children."

"Yes, sir," Reece agreed with annoying enthusiasm.

Claire turned to her booth partner when Bernard Hall left. "Don't say a word."

"What?" Reece raised his palms. "I was only going to point out that you know a lot more about melons than you let on."

She held up the pricing guide Asa had provided. "It says Ambrosia melon right here."

"It doesn't tell you how to know if the melon is ripe."

"Everyone knows that."

"Mr. Hall didn't know that. Neither did I."

"Mr. Hall was testing me. He knew exactly what kind of melons those are, and he knows how to check for ripeness."

"Really?" Reece frowned.

"I worked the farmers market every single Saturday as a teenager. I know all the tricks."

"Makes sense. And I'm guessing you know a lot more about everything else at Ballard Farm than you think you do."

"We'll see." Claire pulled out another flat of melons from beneath the table.

"I've got it," Reece said, intercepting the fruit. "So, what's the history on your farm anyhow?"

She turned to him, suspicion jumping to the forefront. "Why do you ask?"

Reece held up his hands. "Just curious. No ulterior motive. I'm a big fan of family history and heritage, since I have huge gaps in mine."

"According to what I was able to pull from my closemouthed father, my great grandfather made money in the oil fields. He also managed to gamble most of it away. Unbeknownst to him, his wife, the spendthrift daughter of a farmer, took money from their account and squirreled it away when her husband was off doing his roustabout thing. It was enough to start Ballard Farm."

"Real roughnecks, huh?"

"Yes. What about your family?" Claire asked, now curious. Reece had never spoken much about his past. He'd been too angry back then for small talk.

"My mother's father owned the land that Rebel Ranch is on. He forbade my mother from marrying my father and cut his only child out of his will, leaving everything to his grandchildren. We each inherited when we turned twenty-one." He grimaced. "Not nearly as good as your story."

They were silent for a few moments, each unwrapping melons.

"You know, your father sent food over to our house for a long time after my mother passed," Reece said.

"My father had a good heart," Claire said with a sigh. "Ironic, as his heart is what killed him."

"Why, Reece, what are you doing over here?" Saylor Tuttle, the pastor's wife, grinned as she approached the booth. "Who's manning the Rebel Ranch booth?"

Claire turned to Reece. "Rebel Ranch has a booth?"

"Sure. We have ranch literature and cookies with the ranch logo. Violet handles things." He smiled at Mrs. Tuttle. "People don't want to see my face. Violet is much prettier."

The older woman laughed and patted her sky-high, silver bouffant hair. "Oh, honey, don't underestimate yourself. I know plenty of girls in this town who'd stand in line for a smile from you."

Reece shook his head at the words. "That's plain ridiculous."

Claire snuck a peek at his strong profile. Could the man really be that clueless?

"Modest to boot." Mrs. Tuttle winked at Claire. "Good to see you, sweetie. How are you holding up?"

"Everyone in Rebel has been very kind," Claire said.

"This really is a community that comes together." She handed Claire a slip of paper. "Here's my shopping list. We've got a senior dinner coming up at the church."

Claire helped Reece collect the produce in a large box, carefully avoiding any contact.

"May I take that to your car for you, Mrs. Tuttle?" Reece asked when they'd finished.

"You surely may." She nodded to Claire. "Good to see you, dear."

"Thank you. Nice to see you, too."

When they left, Claire glanced around before she pulled the envelope Reece gave her from her pocket and peeked at the check. Reading the amount, she gasped. With this check, she wouldn't have to worry about how she'd pay rent during her exile in Rebel.

She was torn between pride and necessity and couldn't help but feel a bit guilty for second-guessing his motives this morning. Zoe was his daughter, and she'd bite back her pride and accept the check since in Reece's words he was *doing the right thing.*

"Claire?"

Claire looked up to find Daisy at the booth.

"Daisy! Hi, how are you? Where are your children?"

"My grandmother is here for the summer. She gave me the day off."

"How nice."

"What about you?" Daisy asked. "Asa and Nan put you to work already?"

"I volunteered."

"Actually, I heard you were here. I also heard a funny rumor."

"What's that?"

"Reece is working the Ballard booth, too."

"Yes. Nan can be quite persuasive."

Daisy shook her head and a mischievous smile lit up her face. "Reece doesn't do anything he doesn't want to do."

Claire blinked as Daisy's meaning became

clear. "Oh, no. It's not like that," she quickly returned.

Reece was interested in the Ballard booth because of Zoe, nothing more, which was more than enough of a confusing new reality for Claire.

"If you say so," the redhead said. "How long have you known Reece, anyhow?"

"I grew up here, but Reece was way ahead of me in school. He was a senior when I was a freshman in high school."

"But Rebel is so small, surely there weren't that many in each class."

"When you live in a small town, you go to school with all the kids in the half a dozen or so small towns around you."

"Oh, I had no idea." She paused. "Still, I wish I'd known Mitch when he was young. I'm sure both he and Reece were characters."

"I don't remember Mitch, but Reece was very popular."

An understatement. Reece had been the star athlete, and the crush of most of the female population, though he seemed not to care about any of it.

"Are you two talking about me?"

Heat rushed into Claire's cheeks at Reece's comment. She hadn't seen him coming, but his long strides closed the distance quickly and he was behind the table before she could collect herself.

"Were your ears burning?" Daisy asked.

"On fire."

Daisy laughed.

Reece's steady gaze met Claire's and held. She glanced away, taking special care to straighten the stack of Ballard Farm paper bags.

"Claire, I just met your daughter over at the adoption event with Tucker," Daisy said. "She's a sweetheart."

"Thank you."

"Tuck said something about a goat?"

"What?" Claire looked up.

Daisy chuckled. "Tucker is a jokester."

"So it seems," Claire returned.

"Reece, why don't you bring Claire and her daughter to the picnic next Saturday?" Daisy turned to Claire. "We'd love to have you. Will you be in town that long?"

"I'm here for the summer."

Reece's brows shot up at her words.

"Wonderful," Daisy said. She gave Claire and Reece a short salute and a grin. "My work here is done. See you two later, then."

"What picnic?" Claire asked.

"Daisy decided, and rightfully so, that the Rainbolts don't have a single family tradition, except maybe watching the Oklahoma-versus-Texas football game, so she started the annual family picnic last year."

"I'm not family."

"She invited you, so you are now."

Claire stiffened at the words. "That makes no sense. Does your family… Do they know about Zoe?"

"I haven't mentioned anything yet, though I'll have to eventually."

"Not yet," Claire said.

"I get it, and I'm trying to be patient, but I can tell you it's not easy." He paused. "Zoe has lots of family and they all deserve a chance to welcome her."

Lots of family. What would that family think of her keeping Zoe from them all these years?

"So…" Reece glanced around. "You said you're staying." He said the words quietly.

"Do I have a choice?"

"You always have a choice, Claire."

"I'm here for the summer. That's the agreement."

"Fair enough." He held out a hand. "We have a deal, then."

Claire reluctantly put her hand in his and then met his gaze once more.

Reece's eyes were a deep dark blue, like the sea at night. How fitting, since she felt like she had been tossed into the water without a life preserver. Claire swallowed. Was she a strong enough swimmer to tread water for the entire summer? She was about to find out.

Chapter Four

"Mommy, can we live in this house forever?"

Claire turned from the kitchen sink with a peach in one hand and a paring knife in the other. "Why do you want to live here?"

"It's bigger."

"Bigger?"

Claire looked around. She had a point. The large farmhouse kitchen had been designed to her mother's specifications years ago in an attempt to keep her happy. While that plan failed miserably, the kitchen was out of a magazine—albeit a thirty-five-year-old one. It boasted a farmhouse sink and tall white cupboards. Yes, the space could use a face-lift, but still, the appliances, especially the refrigerator, were nicer than hers in her apartment. And most of them hadn't seen much use since her mother left.

Zoe's room here at the farm was twice the size

of hers at home. It was Claire's old room and had a canopy bed.

"It is a nice house," Claire conceded. She glanced around, seeing her homestead through Zoe's eyes.

The construction of the Ballard home had been supervised by her father for his bride. Marta Newton met Davis Ballard at the Tulsa State Fair. It was love at first sight, and that lasted through Claire's fifth birthday.

Her final departure was without explanation, though she promised to return. Her mother would be back. Claire had been sure of it. It was the truth she'd grown up believing in.

It was only in those last months before Marta died of the side effects of alcohol addiction that Claire had gotten to know her mother. She told her only child the real story. The truth that her father had never had the courage to tell her.

Years after she left, Marta sobered up, but with the knowledge that Claire was better off without her. *Her words.* Claire sat at her mother's bedside and listened without judgment. She was a medical professional, and she understood the disease only too well.

Besides, did the truth really matter anymore?

Probably not. It didn't change the fact that Claire had grown up without a mother and with an absentee father.

"Did you have toys when you were a little girl?" Zoe asked.

"What? Hmm?" She looked at Zoe, who sat at the kitchen table drawing, her teeth absently nibbling on her lip in concentration.

"I asked if you had toys when you were a little girl."

"Yes. Of course. Why do you ask?"

"All my toys are at home."

"You brought your coloring books and crayons, and your Polly Pocket dolls."

Zoe shrugged.

"We'll be going to Tulsa next week to get our things for the summer. We can get your toys then. Can you wait that long?"

"I guess." Her dramatic sigh nearly had Claire chuckling. Zoe was a wee bit of a five-year-old diva.

"When I get a minute, I'll look up in the attic for my dollhouse. It has furniture and it would be perfect for your dolls."

Zoe straightened in her seat, eyes widening. "Oh, yes, Mommy. Can we go now?"

"Not right now, sweetie." Claire grabbed a cutting board and began to chop up the soft peaches into small chunks to mash. "I promised Nan I would make peach loaves for the church ladies' bake sale and I have to hurry. Mr. Reece is coming over to see the farm in a little while."

As she spoke, the knife slipped from her wet fingers "Ouch." Crimson blood spurted from a shallow cut. Claire ran her finger under cold water and applied pressure with a clean dish towel.

"Mommy, you're bleeding."

"Tiny cut." Maybe not so tiny, but she didn't want to worry Zoe. "I'm going to go upstairs and look for a bandage." She nodded toward the living room. "Come with me and bring Blue."

"I can watch television?" Zoe perked up. "Come on, Blue."

"Not exactly." Claire turned on her father's big screen TV and slid a videocassette into his VCR.

"What's that?" Zoe hopped on the couch and Blue settled at her feet.

"It's called a VHS tape. This is how kids watched movies in the old days. Grandpa saved all of my favorites. This is a princess movie."

Zoe grinned and settled on the couch. "Thank you."

Claire climbed the oak stairs to the second floor and opened cupboards, looking for supplies. The main bathroom held everything but the first-aid kit that she had bought for her father.

Maybe in his bathroom.

Heart hammering, she opened the door to her father's room. For a few moments, Claire stood with her hand on the doorknob. Finally, she swallowed past a lump in her throat and pushed open the door the rest of the way.

She hadn't been in here since the day of the funeral. Nan had tidied the room and made the bed. For that, Claire was grateful. The room smelled like him. Her father had long ago given up his pipe, but it still rested on his clothes bureau and the scent of vanilla and tobacco lingered in the air, along with the scent of the cedar chips he put in the closet and in his drawers.

In the bathroom, she pulled open the medicine cabinet and froze, her hands moving in slow motion to cover her mouth. Bottles of medication lined the shelf. Medication he never told her about.

Hand shaking, Claire reached for the bottles. They tumbled like dominoes into the sink, the pills rattling as they landed. For a moment, she could only grip the edge of the vanity while the medication names raced through her mind.

Why hadn't he told her? Why had everything been a secret?

Then it struck her. She'd grown up to be just like her father. She'd kept her relationship with Reece a secret. Told no one Zoe was his child. The apple had not fallen far from the Ballard Farm orchard trees.

She carefully replaced the bottles and searched the cupboard below the sink and found a bin filled with supplies. Carefully cleaning and then wrapping her thumb, Claire tidied things up. Tucking the bin under her arm to bring it downstairs, she turned to leave.

Claire stood rooted in the room, unable to move. A man's life had been written between these walls.

When her gaze landed on a professional photo of her mother and father on their wedding day, she moved closer and picked it up. She'd never seen the tarnished silver frame or the photo before. As a teenager, she often came into this room to dust and vacuum. There had been no pictures on the bureau back then.

But here it was, along with a picture of herself as a baby held by her mother. Both photos sat next to the framed picture of herself and Zoe that she'd given her father for Christmas last year.

She examined both images of her mother. With her dark hair and blue eyes, Marta was so lovely.

When she went away, Claire had focused all her attention on her father, seeking reassurance that he wouldn't leave her, as well. She followed him into the orchards, hoping for conversation. Praying he would talk to her. Finally, in later years, she gave up and retreated into books.

The bureau pull jangled when Claire brushed against the metal. Without thinking, she slid open the top drawer, expecting to find his clothes. Instead, she found a photo album.

For several moments, Claire simply stared at the faded ivory faux leather album before she put down the supply bin and gently lifted the volume. She'd never seen the album before. Trepidation tangled with excitement as she settled in her father's favorite chair next to a tall window with the book in her lap.

The view from the window was of Ballard Farm as it bordered Rebel Ranch, with endless neat rows of trees, red clay and mulch. The orchards stretched as far as she could see, the blue Oklahoma sky providing a spectacular backdrop. This was her father's kingdom. His church. Oh, he attended service on Sundays, but the orchards were where he communed with the Lord.

It was a world she'd never quite been privy to. And the pain of that particular rejection might have hurt most of all.

Claire released a sigh and opened the album.

It was a visual document of her parents' marriage and her early childhood with photos of her mother.

Married by a justice of the peace in Oklahoma City, her father wore a suit and her mother a pale yellow dress. She recognized a picture of her uncle Bryant and aunt Dee. Friends really, not family at all. They, too, had passed much too soon.

The smiling faces of her parents in the orchards filled pages of the book. Claire stared, mesmerized, at one of her mother and father together beneath the branches of the fruit trees. For the first time, she understood all that her father lost.

Claire ran finger over the glossy protective plastic as she turned page after page. At the end, she stopped and closed the book. Leaning back in the chair, Claire closed her eyes.

Grief slammed into her like an Oklahoma tornado, pummeling her heart with new aches. Though emotion threatened to spill, she held back tears. She didn't cry about the past anymore. The past was a lot like *what if* and Claire didn't ever go there, because *what if* was a place for dreamers. She was no longer a dreamer.

Reece sniffed the air appreciatively as he stepped into the Ballard kitchen. "Wow. What is that?" A fruity and yeasty aroma told him that he should have had lunch before he came over for the farm tour.

"That depends," Claire said. She had donned oven mitts to remove two loaf pans from the oven. "Is it a good smell or a bad smell?"

"Not a smell, but an aroma. And it's definitely good."

Zoe looked up from the kitchen table, where she carefully replaced crayons in a box. "Mommy made peach bread."

"I thought the peaches weren't ready to pick," Reece said.

"I used frozen ones from last year."

"I'm impressed." The bread wasn't all that impressed him. It was the life she'd created for Zoe—the scene he had stepped into in this kitchen. He'd longed for this in his own life.

"Don't be," she scoffed. "The first batch was a fail. I grabbed baking soda instead of powder. And the second batch was disastrous. I lost track of how many eggs I added and had to start over."

"*You*, distracted?"

"Don't look so surprised. I have a zillion things on my mind right now."

"Yeah, I can relate."

Claire met his gaze, her expression doubtful.

Why was it he felt like the bad guy in this situation? In truth, he hadn't had a good night's sleep since he found out Zoe was his daughter. He had so many things going through his head. He wanted to share with his brothers and call his sister, Kate. He wanted to shout to the world that an amazing thing had happened. Despite his long list of shortcomings and his best self-defeating behavior, he was the father to an amazing child.

Again, he glanced over at Zoe, who rewarded

him with a bright smile. For a moment, he caught his breath as he considered all the Zoe smiles that he'd never seen.

She was a wonderful kid, and it killed him to keep her parentage a secret from his family—to keep it from Zoe. His mother's death, followed by his baby brother Levi's, gave all the Rainbolts a deeper appreciation for family than most folks.

"We better get going." Claire removed her gloves and nodded toward the door. "Zoe, put on your sneakers, honey."

Reece did a double take at the gauze wrap on Claire's thumb.

"What happened to you?"

"A little run-in with a paring knife. It's nothing." She shook her head.

"That's a lot of bandage for nothing."

"I'm fine."

"Have you had a tetanus shot?"

Claire frowned. "I'm a nurse. I've got this covered."

"Yeah, right. Sorry."

Again, she nodded toward the door. "Asa is waiting for us in the barn. Shall we get going?"

"Yes, ma'am." Reece almost laughed out loud. She was a lot bossier than he remembered.

"Can we take Blue with us?" Zoe asked.

"Not this time," Claire said. "We have work to do."

Blue whined from his bed on the kitchen floor.

"Sorry, Blue." Zoe rubbed his head and followed Reece out the door, smiling. She was always happy. How did Claire manage to raise such a good-natured kid? Once they were outside, she skipped ahead down the gravel road leading to the machine barn.

"Have you had a chance to review the books?" Reece asked.

"Barely. The accountant sent me the tax forms from the last few years. The farm is staying inches ahead of itself. Nothing remarkable." She paused. "The thing is there is no real financial cushion, either. Mother Nature cooperating through the end of autumn is essential."

"Mind if I look things over?"

"Your accountant?"

"No. Me." Reece bristled. He ought to be used to being underestimated by now. Somehow, with Claire, the sting was back and reminding him that most folks figured he was a pretty-faced cowboy with little upstairs. "I may not have a degree, but as it turns out I'm good with math." Reece couldn't help looking down the path toward Zoe.

"I didn't mean—" Claire began to backpedal.

"Doesn't matter. Just send them over when you get a chance."

"Of course."

They kept walking. The only sound was Zoe kicking a rock.

"How old is Asa?" Reece finally broke the silence.

"A few years younger than my father. So around sixty."

"Ever thought about bringing on some younger management?"

"I haven't thought about anything, Reece," she said, her tone defensive. "But I can tell you this, Nan and Asa practically raised me. They'll always have a home here at Ballard Farm."

"Not if you walk away."

Claire opened her mouth, about to speak, and then fell silent.

He wasn't going to sugarcoat things. Not now. Not ever. Walking away from Ballard Farm had serious repercussions, and he refused to give her an easy out. Not when her future was entwined with his through their child.

"Look," he finally said. "I get your loyalty to the Turners. But when it comes to business, you have to manage with your head leading and your heart giving opinions that may or may not have any bearing in reality. This is a tough economy."

"So you're suggesting that letting Asa and Nan go is what will save the farm?"

"I didn't say that," Reece returned.

"It seems to me you did."

"Have you ever run your own business?"

"Well, no. I'm an RN. First, I was a nurse aid, then when I graduated I was a floor nurse and currently I'm a supervisor."

"And your father put you through college."

"It's not like I had a silver spoon in my mouth. I worked hard, and I had excellent grades."

"But you've never been up against the wall. You have never been in a position where you have had to decide between bad and worse."

"Excuse me. I'm the single mother of a five-year-old. I understand difficult decisions too well."

"Claire, you are a single mother by choice."

She released a soft gasp and turned to be sure Zoe hadn't heard the exchange.

Reece grimaced, remorseful. "I'm sorry. That didn't come out right." He took a slow breath. The conversation was getting out of control and the last thing he wanted was to create more friction between him and the mother of his child.

"I'm not criticizing you, Claire. I'm telling you that you need to step back and be objective. The future of Ballard Farm will ride on what we do in the next weeks and months."

"I thought you wanted me to keep Ballard Farm."

"I do. But in order to do that, you may have to make decisions that will not be easy."

"Asa and Nan aside, what else?"

"It looks to me like this place has been held together by duct tape."

"That's not true." The words seemed a knee-jerk response without conviction. She was disagreeing because the observation came from him. If she really took a good look around, she'd have to agree with his assessment.

"The house needs a good paint job and some updates. The barns and the fences all need maintenance."

Claire was silent, staring straight ahead, her face impossible to read.

"How many workers does the farm support?" he asked.

"I couldn't tell you. I do know my father has laid off workers in the last years. Asa—"

"Asa can't do it all."

Her blue eyes were fierce when her gaze met his. "I was going to say that Asa manages the orchard and greenhouses and the machinery. My father handled the retail and wholesale sales."

"The two of them. That's it? Was that to save money?"

"Probably, but more than likely it's because my father is—was a micromanager who buried himself in his work."

Reece was beginning to draw the same conclusion.

"What about the produce market? That's probably the only thing I'm familiar with." He looked in the direction of the red clapboard building—an oversized fruit stand that was used to sell produce directly to the public. But a quick glance said that even the market could do with a fresh coat of paint.

"Nan manages that."

He nodded. "Next week, I'm going to send Willard Cornell over here to evaluate the property and we'll take it from there."

"Take what? Where?" Claire asked. "And who is Willard Cornell?"

"Willard is one of my trusted ranch hands. He'll let me know what needs to be done and then you and I can discuss."

As they approached the open doors of the machine barn, Asa Turner stepped out to greet them. In overalls and a green John Deere cap, the production manager smiled when Claire reached out to offer him a hug.

Reece's eyes widened at the gesture. Claire was not a hugger.

When Asa offered Reece a hand, he accepted.

"Reece. Good to see you. You're doing a mighty fine job next door."

"I can't take all the credit. Rebel Ranch is a family operation."

Asa chuckled. "Don't be modest. It doesn't take

a genius to figure out who's in charge over there. Keep up the good work."

"Thank you, sir." Reece nodded at the unexpected praise.

"Mommy, I see a rabbit." All heads turned as Zoe raced down a row of peach trees.

"Excuse me, gentlemen," Claire said as she followed her daughter. "Hang on, Zoe."

"Glad to have you helping at Ballard Farm," Asa said once Claire was out of earshot.

"I'm not so sure Claire's glad," Reece murmured.

"Yeah. I couldn't help but hear you two talking. Butting heads about something?"

"Pretty much everything," Reece admitted.

Asa laughed. "She's as stubborn as her father."

"That might very well be true," Reece said. He cocked his head in time to see both Zoe and Claire duck between the trees.

"What's the harvest schedule look like here?" Reece asked.

"Next week we start with the peaches. Most everything in the greenhouses are ready. We'll see harvest at regular intervals now through September."

"Who helps you with that?"

"We have a half dozen seasonal workers coming in for the next three months."

"Claire and I want to participate."

"You do?"

"Good managers learn the business from the ground up," Reece said.

"I couldn't agree with you more," Asa said. He began to stroll through the peach orchard. "Our biggest concern right now is the weather. Been monitoring a storm off the coast of Texas. We should be fine for peaches. Won't affect the apples too much. But if the pecans flood, we could lose the entire harvest."

Reece offered a nod as he filed away the information.

Asa paused. "What about your ranch, Reece? Who will manage things if you're over here?"

"Good a time as any to let Mitch run the show. He's been pestering me to take a little time off."

"This isn't exactly time off." The older man laughed. "Far from it."

"It's different work. I'm kind of excited to learn about the farm."

"Are you? I guess you know Claire doesn't share your enthusiasm. Though I have to tell you, there was a time when she did."

"What changed?"

"Claire needed more than her daddy could give her. She had to compete against the orchards for his attention." He shook his head slowly. "Davis was a good man, but locked up so tight, even his only child couldn't get in. A shame, too."

"Yeah, it is." Reece reached out and touched a peach. The blushing fruit sat in his palm.

"Colored up and ready to harvest," Asa said.

"Because it's red?"

"Nah, the shade of red only indicates the variety. Look at that gold color. That indicates ripeness. We'll be starting harvest middle of next week and repeat until the fruit are picked and processed."

"How long does that last?"

"The semifreestone are the first to ripen and then in mid-July the freestone will be ready. Makes for a successive harvest."

"All of these trees?"

"There's a large pick-your-own section near the market building."

"Where else do you sell the fruit?" Reece asked.

"Ballard Farm Market is our primary outlet and local grocers."

They walked through the neat rows as Asa explained the production process, pointing out the new trees that had been planted this year.

"Peach trees only provide twelve years or so of fruit. So we're always planting new ones."

Reece nodded. "If you could change anything about the farm, what would it be?"

"Aw, I don't want to cast aspersions on Davis."

"I'm asking your opinion. The terms of Davis's

will put all of us in a unique position. I have a responsibility to assess everything from all sides to determine the future of Ballard Farm."

"You're going to sell?" Asa pulled off his cap and ran a hand through his sparse shock of gray hair before slapping the hat back on.

"Not my plan, but I'm a businessman first and foremost."

"Fair enough." He nodded. "Fact is I've always thought we should capitalize on the Ballard Farm brand name. Like some of those big outfits over there in Porter. Why don't we have a shop to sell merchandise? Why aren't we producing our own cider and other apple products?"

"You tell me."

"Davis didn't want to go commercial, plain and simple. I honored his decision and I understood. Yes, we're a small operation. But there's nothing wrong with good marketing. A web page and a presence on social media goes a long way."

"I agree. And you've given me a lot to think about. I'll do some research and we can talk again."

"I'd like that. And, Reece, don't get me wrong, Davis launched several great projects, like the downtown Rebel Farmers Market. And he always donated bushels of fruit that were auctioned off to support the community center. He also funded a scholarship for our local Future Farmers organization."

"I didn't know that."

"That's because he believed the right hand shouldn't know what the left is doing."

"Wise man."

"Yup. Mostly." Asa reached for a stick on the ground and winced as he stood.

"You okay?" Reece asked.

"Oh, yeah, sure. Back's been giving me a bit of trouble."

"Sorry to hear that."

"What are you gonna do?" He shrugged. "I keep getting older, whether I like it or not."

"Ever thought of retiring?"

"Farmers don't retire, son. They just go to seed."

Reece froze at the comment and then he grinned, realizing the words were a joke that nearly sailed right over his head. "Thanks for taking the time to explain things to me, Asa."

"Glad to have you on board, son."

"What time do you want us here to pick peaches?"

"Should have the grader part we need in tomorrow and we'll be up and running in time to start on Wednesday. We work sunrise to sunset for those first few days. Nan will bring lunch and dinner for the picking crew."

"That's a long day. You may be a tougher task-master than I am."

Asa chuckled. "Welcome to my world."

"What are you two talking about?" Claire asked as she approached. Zoe followed behind.

"Picking," Reece said. "We report for duty on Wednesday morning."

Claire turned to Reece. "When I was little, Asa gave me a quarter for every bushel I dumped into the collection containers."

"Bet you wish you had those quarters now," Asa said. "You've accumulated quite a few in your time."

"Maybe it's time for Zoe to earn quarters," Reece said.

Claire's expression as she turned to find her daughter said she wholly disagreed. "Zoe, come on. We're leaving."

"Thanks again, Asa," Reece said.

"Anytime. We can use a smart fella like you around here."

As they headed back to the house, Claire shook her head.

"What?" he asked.

"You won him over. That isn't easy."

"Oh?" Reece returned. He found himself inor-dinately pleased. After spending a lifetime being on the wrong side of most everything, it was nice to hear words of praise from an old-timer like Asa Turner.

"And you're looking forward to picking peaches, too, aren't you?" Claire asked.

"I take it you are not."

"It's a novelty for you. Not for me. I'm only doing this because I promised." Her steps quickened.

"Wouldn't want you to actually enjoy the farm," he said to her retreating form.

Claire ignored his comment, her gaze on Zoe. When she reached the house, she turned and had a stiff smile on her face. "I guess that's it for today. Thanks for coming by."

She was dismissing him. Reece rubbed a hand over his face. He couldn't seem to catch a break with Claire. Every time he thought they were on even ground, things got real bumpy. "You and Zoe will be at Daisy's, right?" he asked.

"Yes."

"May I pick you up?"

"Not necessary." She waved a hand. "We'll see you there."

"Are you leaving, Mr. Reece?" Zoe called from behind them.

"I am, but I'll see you tomorrow."

She ran up to him and held out her hand "Here. For you. I found it under a tree."

"What is this?" he asked, stooping down to her level.

Her fingers opened, revealing a smooth and flat stone in her palm. "It's a heart. See?"

"Yeah, I guess it is." The stone looked nothing like a heart, but it touched him all the same. "Wow. Very nice. Are you sure you don't want to keep it?"

"You're my friend. I want you to take it."

Emotion kicked Reece in the gut at the earnest expression in her eyes. He longed to tell her that he was her father. "Thank you, Zoe," he said softly.

"You're making friends all over the place," Claire said.

He looked up and met Claire's gaze, but once again was unable to decipher what she was thinking. "Some folks think I'm a likable guy."

"Huh, how about that," she murmured.

"Until tomorrow, Claire," Reece said. "Bye, Zoe." He tossed the stone in the air and caught it before slipping it in his pocket and heading to his truck. One step at a time. That's all he could hope for.

Chapter Five

"That's it. I'm staying home." Claire said the words aloud. She grabbed another piece of mail from a stack on the kitchen table and slit open the envelope. Yet another bill that was overdue because there was no one to open the farm mail in her father's absence.

She glanced at the clock and ran her fingers over her lips. Two hours until the picnic. Ugh.

Why was it that going to a social gathering always seemed like a good idea until you actually had to go? She had a long history of not being a social person. Even now, her life consisted of Zoe and work. On a rare occasion, she had coffee or lunch with coworkers. Even then, they only talked about work.

"And I definitely do not need the stress," she murmured.

"I heard that."

Claire turned around in her chair. Nan stood at the screen door.

"Mind if I come in?"

"You are always welcome here."

"You're talking yourself out of the picnic?"

For a moment, Claire considered denying the charge, but Nan's expression said she wasn't having any of it.

"You can't stay home, Claire. Zoe is all excited about playing with Hazel and Ginger." Nan paused. "Although, I suppose you could always let her go with Reece."

"Without me? No way. What should I wear to a family picnic?"

"Oh, anything goes."

"What about this?" Claire stood and reached for two delivery boxes on the far side of the kitchen table. She lifted a simple flowered summer dress in shades of blue from the wrappings.

"Did you buy that online?"

"I did. It arrived yesterday afternoon." She pulled the other box close. "Sandals, too."

Nan stared at the boxes in awe. "I can't even imagine shopping for clothes from my computer. But it sure is tempting, given the lack of selection in the shops in Rebel."

"It's scary easy. I may never shop in a physical store again."

"Huh, isn't that something?" Bemused, Nan

touched the fabric of the dress, evaluating the stitching on the straps. "This is very nice, Claire."

Claire, too, examined the outfit. "Are you sure it isn't too…"

"Too what?"

"Pearls and Tabu perfume. I don't want to go dressed as my grandmother."

Laughter spilled from the older woman. "Not at all. It's a sundress and it's adorable."

"I wasn't shooting for adorable." Claire paused. What exactly was she looking for? Certainly not to turn Reece's eye. No, that was a road she would never journey down again. Though her pride could use a boost. And it would be nice to let the cowboy know what he'd missed out on when he dumped her.

"You'll impress everyone, Claire," Nan said.

"I don't want to impress. I want to blend in." She offered a small smile. "Basically, I want to stay home."

"Some things never change," Nan said with a laugh. "You are so like your father. He always said that anywhere that required him to change out of his overalls wasn't worth going."

"I can see his point."

"Are you going with Reece?" Nan asked.

"Reece will be there and so will I. I prefer to attend on my own. That way I can pretend I'm not being held hostage by Reece Rainbolt." She groaned and pushed her hair back from her face. "Held hostage for the summer and I don't like it one bit."

"That's pretty strong. You can say no. No to today. No to it all."

"It's not that easy. Reece has custody of Zoe and Ballard Farm as leverage. He's making nice as long as I am."

"Perhaps you're exaggerating a little."

"Oh, no. Those are definitely the facts. But the Rainbolts are Zoe's family. In all fairness, she deserves what I didn't have—a relationship with an extended family. Or in my case, any family."

"Does it help if I tell you that Daisy really likes you? Her journey isn't much different from your own. You have an ally in that woman."

"I'm not sure anything will help, but having an ally is a good thing. I have precious few."

"If you'd let yourself, you'd have more friends in Rebel than you have fingers and toes. You could find a place for yourself and Zoe here. A good life."

Claire shook her head. "There are too many memories."

"Make new memories."

"Maybe," she murmured. "The trouble is when I'm in Tulsa I forget everything that brought me to today. I let it go. The minute I cross the county line into Osage County my mind starts to bring up everything from yesterday. It's a losing battle."

"You're wrong. You simply need to call on the Lord when you feel that way. His compassion. His mercy. His love. They are new every morning." She nodded. "You can't whine that you're parched when the living water is right there for you to take."

"Am I whining?" Claire asked. She held up a hand. "Don't answer that." No, she did not need an answer, because the moment she said it, Claire knew it was true. She'd been whining ever since she left Edwin Sanders's office.

Something had to change, and she feared it was probably going to have to be her.

Thirty minutes later, the conversation with Nan continued to loop through Claire's mind as she headed toward Daisy and Mitch's house on the outskirts of Rebel. Could new memories possibly dim the light of the past? She knew fear was standing between her and moving forward, but right now, recognizing the problem was not getting her any closer to fixing it.

"I get to play with Ginger and Hazel," Zoe chanted over and over from the back seat.

"You do. And there will be more kids than that. Mr. Reece's brother Mr. Mitch has seven children. One of them is starting kindergarten this fall, just like you."

"Who?"

"His name is Sam."

"Sam. Sam. Sam," Zoe repeated. "Mommy?"

"Hmm?"

"Can I have brothers and sisters?"

"I, um…" Claire's gaze shot to the rearview mirror. Zoe was absently humming and playing with a doll.

"Did you hear me, Mommy?"

"I did." She gripped the steering wheel and took a deep breath. "Maybe someday you can." Even as she said the words, Claire chastised herself for making promises she definitely could not keep.

Life was good just the way it was. Well, maybe not right now, but normally. They had a routine. Routines and structure were a very good thing. It had served her well since Zoe was born. No surprises, no chaos and definitely no Reece Rainbolt.

Claire frowned. Except Reece was not going away and she hadn't yet figured out how he was going to fit into the new normal.

She steered her hybrid up the drive toward the big yellow farmhouse. The drive was long and graveled, which was a good thing as it was filled with six or seven vehicles.

Claire tensed. Why had she thought family picnic meant small and intimate?

Mitch and Daisy's home was even larger than

the Ballard Farm homestead. A lovely wrap-around porch circled the front and side and continued on to the back of the house.

Even from the drive, she could see the backyard was huge. The flaps of a large canopy waved in the breeze. Beneath the canopy, long picnic tables with checkerboard tablecloths had been set up.

"Mommy, this is a big party."

"Yes, it is," Claire said softly. "A big party."

Claire grabbed the cardboard box that held her contribution for the picnic meal from the back seat. She hadn't dared step into baking territory when invited to a baker's house, so she'd made a salad. Everyone at work raved about her spinach salad with pecans, cranberries and feta cheese. Though, now she found herself second-guessing that decision. Was it the right choice for this crowd? Maybe she should leave it in the car.

"May I help you with that?"

Reece.

"Sure. Thanks." When she faced him, his expression registered surprise, before he scooped the box from her arms.

"Nice dress."

Heat warmed Claire's face as she willed her heart to cease its silly flutter and her breathing to return to normal. This was Reece. It was a

nice gesture on his part. That was all. "Um…
Thank you."

"What do you have in here?" he asked.

"A salad and the fixings. I haven't put the
dressing on yet."

"Great. I'm a big salad fan."

Claire frowned. "I took you for a steak guy."

"I like steak *and* salad." He offered a slow
shake of his head, the dark blue eyes almost dis-
appointed as he stared at her intently. "You think
you know me, Claire. But you don't."

"Mr. Reece. Mr. Reece. Wait for me." Zoe
scrambled out of her car seat and straightened
her pink dress.

"Zoe-girl. You look beautiful."

"I do?" She glanced down at her frock.

"Prettiest girl here."

Zoe's eyes lit up like she'd never heard such
words. "I am?"

"You are." He shifted the box to one arm and
held out his hand. Zoe put her small fingers in
his big palm. "Come on. Let's go find everyone."

Okay, Claire conceded, bonus points for Reece.
A little girl's self-esteem soars when she's the
apple of her daddy's eye. And Reece just turned
on the lightbulb in Zoe's heart. Claire was grateful.

The three of them walked toward the house,

Claire a step behind, still a bit stunned by Reece's words to Zoe.

Claire turned at the sound of the clink of horseshoes in the distance. She recognized several people playing, Tucker and Mitch Rainbolt among them. Behind the game, a small orchard spanned the back of the property.

"I thought your family was small," Claire said. "This is quite a get-together."

"Some are family by association."

"Still, I am looking at a lot of people."

"This is a small gathering by my standards. Big would be the shindig we had at Rebel Ranch right before you arrived. Every year we herald in the summer with a real old-fashioned hoedown for the ranch guests and most of the business owners in town. A kickoff to the busy tourist season."

Claire smiled. She couldn't help recalling a time or two that her father hosted one of those at the end of the season to celebrate a good harvest.

"Mommy, there's Ginger and Hazel. Can I go play with them on the swings?"

"Yes. You may." Claire moved up the porch steps. "But I have to be able to see you from right here."

"She'll be fine—" Reece began.

Claire jerked back at his words. "Did you hear me, Zoe?"

"Yes, Mommy."

"Sorry," Reece murmured as Zoe skipped off. "I guess I'm not real clear on the chain of command yet."

She began to respond and then stopped herself. What could she say?

Co-parenting. The word slammed into her. Just when she thought she was getting to know the rules of the game, the ground shifted. Something else for her and Reece to discuss. The list was becoming very long.

"Claire, you made it." Daisy greeted them on the porch. "Did you two come together?"

She glanced at Reece awkwardly. "Um, no."

"Come on in," Daisy said. Her face lit up at the sight of the box. "What's in there?"

"Claire brought a salad. And it must be a huge one," Reece said, "because this box is heavy." He feigned effort as he carried the box in the house and slid it on a farmhouse kitchen table that was surrounded by five chairs and a highchair.

"That's just the glass serving bowl," Claire returned.

"I'm grateful you brought salad. I have a veggie platter but no one else brought greens. So thank you."

"Sure. Just toss on the vinaigrette when you're ready to serve. I brought two bottles."

"Wonderful," Daisy said. She stirred a pot on the stove as they spoke.

Claire looked around. She did remember this house but couldn't quite place how. "The Kendalls lived here, right?"

"Yeah," Reece said. "Good memory."

"Whatever happened to them?"

"Retired to Arizona long ago. Daisy bought the house almost two years ago."

"It looks amazing."

"It does now. The trouble with old houses is that you have to keep up the maintenance. Mitch called in all his favors to get everything on our list completed before our latest family members arrived."

"Where are the babies?" Claire asked.

"They're in the yard with my grandmother. Probably sleeping."

From outside a hoot went up. "This is a noisy group," Claire said.

"I have a noisy household. We've raised the kids to be able to sleep through anything."

"I never thought about it. That's very wise." This was a whole new world to Claire. She only had one child. Though she couldn't fathom juggling more than Zoe, a part of her envied Daisy and her houseful.

"Imagine trying to keep all these kids quiet," Daisy said with a laugh.

Reece cleared his throat and glanced outside through the screen door. "I think this is the part of the conversation where I excuse myself. I'm going to find my brothers."

"Go ahead," Daisy said. "We'll be along soon."

"How can I help?" Claire asked. Her gaze spanned the kitchen.

"Everything is done. I'll put your salad in the fridge until we get the call that the burgers and hot dogs are ready. Mitch is on the grill so it shouldn't be too long."

"How about if I wash these dishes while you finish up?"

"That would be great. Thanks." Daisy raised a hand. "Before I forget, I want to invite you and Zoe to Sam's birthday party. It's a week after the Fourth of July. He's turning six and wants a pizza party. We rented a meeting room at the community center and ordered pizza."

"You're amazing, Daisy." Claire washed and rinsed a large serving bowl. "You run a bakery, have seven children and you're hosting another party."

"Not me. Mitch is helping. We're doing our best to experience the childhood we never had by having excessive fun with our children. To that end, it takes very little for us to find a good excuse for a get-together."

"Both you and Mitch had childhood challenges…"

"MIA parents on both of our family trees."

"Reece?"

"His father took off. I probably should let Reece speak for himself. But trust me, it's an epidemic that stops here. We're determined to let our kids be kids, and that includes Mitch and me."

"That reminds me of that bumper sticker," Claire said.

"It's never too late to have a happy childhood." Daisy laughed. "Exactly."

"Aunt D, may we set up the badminton game?" A child of about ten spoke through the screen door.

"Sure, sweetie. But make sure there are no babies near the area when you play."

"Thank you."

Daisy turned to Claire. "That was Seth. He and his sister Grace are the eldest. Fraternal twins. We lost my sister and her husband over two years ago."

Claire's heart ached at the explanation. "Remind me never to complain about one child. And yet, it doesn't explain how organized you are. You're spinning six plates at one time."

Daisy laughed. "It's all done with smoke and mirrors and a few apps on my phone."

Behind them, someone cleared their throat. Claire turned to see Reece had entered the kitchen again.

"Got a minute?" he asked Claire.

"Go ahead, Claire. I'll be out shortly."

She wiped her hands on a towel and followed him out the door and down the steps. "What is it?" Her gaze scanned the yard. "Is Zoe all right?"

"At your twelve o'clock. See her on the tree swing. She's having a great time." Reece took Claire by the arm and led her to a secluded area near the driveway. "There's something I should tell you."

"Uh-oh."

"I had to let my family know about the will, since it now involves Rebel Ranch. While I manage the ranch, I only own a fourth of the business."

"I see."

"Do you?"

"Maybe not," she admitted.

"In five years you never told anyone that I'm Zoe's father?"

"No. No one."

"I sure don't get that, but I can tell you this much. The Rainbolts don't keep secrets and I'm going to need their help while I spend time at Ballard Farm."

"Why are you just telling me now?"

"I forgot until Mitch said something to me a minute ago."

"Did they have questions?"

"Oh, yeah. Plenty of questions." Reece nodded. "Kate is here for the weekend, so we held a business meeting. Reviewed the books and the plans for the rest of the year. I told them I'd answer all questions in due time and asked everyone to trust me for now."

Trust him. And they would because Reece had proved to them he was trustworthy. A concept Claire still grappled with.

"Okay." She wrapped her arm around herself, suddenly chilly despite the warm June day. "Was there anything else you shared?"

"No. But I want to. You know that."

"We agreed. When the time is right."

Jaw tense, and his eyes intent, Reece pushed back the brim of his cowboy hat. "When will that be Claire?"

"I've only been in Rebel for two weeks. Is there a rush?"

"Maybe to me there is. Two weeks is a long time when you find out you're a father to a five-year-old. I want to get started being Zoe's father, especially since you're only going to be here for the summer."

"Zoe may not be ready."

He released a breath that said his patience was wearing thin. "This isn't about Zoe. This is your issue."

Claire stiffened. "I don't have issues."

"No?" He frowned. "What have you told her about me?"

"You know. That you're Mr. Reece and you live next door."

Reece shook his head. "Claire. I'm her father. Haven't you had her to yourself long enough?"

She could only step back at the accusation. Then she glanced around, growing more uncomfortable. "Could we please discuss this elsewhere?"

"Fine. But we are going to discuss it. I want bragging rights, Claire."

"Parenting is more than bragging rights."

"I know that. I'm an uncle times nine. I'm a good uncle, too. Involved. Contrary to what you think, I'm going to be a good father."

"It was never about what you're capable of, Reece." No. It was always about him walking away.

"Reece?"

Both Reece and Claire turned to see a beautiful young woman in a denim skirt and a pretty red T-shirt. Her dark hair was pulled into a high ponytail and the ends had been dipped in purple. A wide smile reached the bluest eyes. Eyes just like Zoe's.

"Kate. This is Claire Ballard." Reece's stiff stance relaxed and a warm smile brightened his face as he spoke. "Claire, this is my little sister—my only sister—Kate."

Claire, too, relaxed. "Oh, I've heard a lot about you."

"You have?" Kate's gaze went immediately to Reece.

"Cut it out," Reece said. "I always brag on you. A female rodeo clown and a buckle-winning barrel racer."

"Did Reece ever mention that I got into rodeo because he was my idol?" Kate asked. She playfully socked her brother in the arm. "I was ten when he took off for the circuit. That was when I decided I wanted to be just like my big brother."

"You're far better than your big brother."

"Not so. Though, like him, I'm not competing much anymore. That's what happens when you get old."

"Right," Reece said. "She'll be thirty this year. I'm the old guy in this crowd at thirty-seven."

"You're not as old as Mitch," Kate said.

Reece chuckled. "That only makes me feel slightly better."

Claire enjoyed the warm exchange between the siblings. She found herself almost jealous of the loving bond between them. Most of all, she found herself again confused by the Reece Rainbolt who stood before her and the callous man who broke her heart six years ago.

His sister turned to Claire. "Enough about me. What about you, Claire? I heard you lost your daddy. I'm so sorry. We all loved Mr. Ballard."

"Thank you, Kate."

"And that little girl with Tucker's twins is yours?"

"Zoe. Yes."

"She's beautiful. You'll have to bring her by the ranch sometime. I was in the saddle by the time I was five."

Claire shot a glance at Reece.

He stepped back and gave an adamant shake of his head. "I did not coach her."

"Uh-oh. Did I step in the middle of a cow paddy with this subject?" Kate asked.

"Simply a friendly discussion between neighbors," Claire said. "For the record, I do plan to take Zoe to the ranch. Soon." Because maybe making a few concessions would ease the tension between her and Reece.

Reece's brows rose in surprise. "I'd like that. Every little girl should learn to ride."

In the distance, someone called Kate's name. "If you'll excuse me, that's Tucker. He no doubt needs me to be his horseshoe partner."

"Are you serious about Zoe visiting the ranch?" Reece asked when Kate stepped away.

"I said yes. Now can we just enjoy the day?"

"Sure. Would you like to play a rousing game of horseshoes?"

"Why don't I watch first? A wise man once said you should never get drawn into a game where you don't know all the rules. Besides, I don't want to commit to something I can't win."

Reece burst out laughing. "That's pure Claire Ballard."

"It is not. I read that on the back of a cereal box. But it applies."

"Whatever you say. But winning isn't everything, Claire." He shook his head. "Sometimes it's about having the courage to play the game."

She stared at him. "I need to read more cereal boxes if we're going to continue this conversation."

"In the meantime," he said. "I'm going to grab Dr. Jena to play a round."

"Dr. Jena? The other vet from the animal adoption event?"

"That's her. She runs the Rebel Vet and Rescue with my brother Tucker." He nodded toward the horseshoe area. "The petite one with the oversized glasses."

"Are she and Tucker an item?"

"Naw, they've been close friends for years. Tucker isn't ready for a relationship."

"How long has it been?"

"Hazel and Ginger were babies when they lost their mama."

Claire sighed. "Tucker juggles two children and Daisy and Mitch seven. I'm in awe of your family." The Rainbolts constantly set a new standard for parenting and she was starting to realize what a lightweight she was.

"We're there for each other. That's what family is for, Claire. You're not supposed to do it all by yourself."

"Well played, Rainbolt." She hadn't missed how Reece had neatly circled the conversation back around to the topic at hand.

Reece raised both hands, palms up. "Hey, I'm just sayin'."

Yes. He was just saying, and he might be right, too. Though, she would not hand him that victory quite yet. What happened when the Rainbolts found out she'd kept Zoe from them for the last five years? They might just decide to roll up the welcome mat. Claire wasn't ready to test their hospitality. Not today, at least.

"And there's Baby." Reece pulled his pickup into the Ballard Farm drive and parked. The black-and-white-spotted Holstein stood in Claire's backyard with her face to the sun, her tail swishing rhythmically. She'd outlived most dairy cows her age and deserved her time in the sunshine. Just not in this particular yard.

"Tell me again why we have a dairy cow who keeps escaping?" Willard asked from the passenger seat.

"Because my brother can't say no."

"You're talking about Tucker, but it seems to me he takes after you. In my opinion, both of you fellas have a problem saying no."

"Which is why nobody asked your opinion."

Willard reached for his toolbox on the floor of the truck. "There is that."

"Now can you get Baby home and get moving with fixing the fences?"

"Yes, sir, boss. I'm on it. But I can tell you, Baby won't cooperate. That cow plain doesn't like me."

"If you'll talk sweet to her she'll follow you anywhere."

Willard stepped away, grumbling beneath his breath. "Sweet-talking an old cow. My job description just hit an all-time low."

Crossing the gravel drive, Reece strode up to the Ballard house, where he braced himself for another round with Claire. Seemed it was one step forward and two steps back with the woman. Saturday's picnic was no exception. He'd gained some ground, but not much.

He'd reviewed the situation carefully in the last

two weeks since she arrived. Most folks liked him. In fact, everyone liked him. As a man of God, a brother and a businessman, he went out of his way to be kind and obliging. Yet, whenever he was around Claire, there was an underlying animosity on her part that he couldn't overcome, and it had nothing to do with his lack of pedigree. Her gaze remained wary and the bulletproof armor was always in place. Sure, he'd messed up six years ago. Why couldn't she see that he was a changed man?

He took a deep breath and knocked on the door.

"Reece? Was I expecting you?" Claire's face when she pulled open the door reflected confusion.

He couldn't help but notice how cute she looked in an old T-shirt and jeans. When she pushed back her hair, it only served to make the messy bun on top of her head wobble. Reece tried not to smile.

"I was in the area and thought I'd see if you have a minute to discuss a few things," he said in his most businesslike voice.

"You live in the area."

He froze. Trust Claire to take him off guard. "Yeah. I do. Do you have a few minutes?"

"What do you want to discuss, Reece?"

"You've got that suspicious look in your eyes again, Claire."

"And you've got a guilty look in yours," she returned quickly.

"Look, Baby got loose again. She's in your yard now. Willard will be here both today and tomorrow working on the fences."

"I'll reimburse you for that."

"Nope. Those are my fences now, too, and they need to be fixed. Willard is my best fence mender. That's why he's on the payroll."

"He's on Rebel Ranch payroll."

"Doesn't matter. We pierced the veil when we left the attorney's office."

"There's a baby in our backyard?" Zoe asked.

"Baby is a cow," Claire said.

"We have a cow in our backyard?" Zoe practically squeaked. "I want to see the cow, Mommy."

"Stay right where you are, young lady," Claire said, as Zoe pushed against the screen door.

Zoe poked her head under Claire's arm with Blue thumping along right behind her. Child and dog peered out the screen door. Once he spotted the cow, Blue howled at the sight.

"Hush, Blue," Claire said to the Lab. She gave him a reassuring pat.

"What's that man doing with the cow?" Zoe asked.

Reece turned. Willard stood behind Baby's shoulder, and step by laborious step, he guided her with a gloved hand to the other side of the fence. Occasionally, he'd stop and whisper something to the bovine.

"He's taking Baby back home," Reece said.

"What is he saying in her ear?" Claire asked.

"He's whispering sweet words. Baby won't move unless she likes you."

"Seriously?" Claire asked.

"Serious as can be."

"Baby lives with you, Mr. Reece?"

He laughed. "She lives on the ranch."

"Baby sure walks slow," Zoe said.

"Yeah, cows walk about two miles an hour on a good day and since Baby has issues with Willard, it's going to take even longer."

Claire cleared her throat. "You said there was another reason you're here?"

"Yeah. I tried to find you at church yesterday, but you peeled rubber out of that parking lot."

"I observed the speed limit."

"Mr. Reece, we saw you at church but Mommy said we had to hurry home."

Claire's face pinked. "We *were* in a hurry."

He snorted. "A hurry to avoid me."

"That's not true completely true." Claire put her hand on Zoe's head. "Sweetie, why don't you go upstairs and bring me the laundry from your hamper. Put it on the washing machine. Please and thank you."

"Oh-kay."

Reece glanced up at the cloudless blue sky. "Nice day. There's even a breeze."

"Are you giving me a weather report?" Claire asked.

"Just passing the time until you get around to inviting me in," he said. Or maybe she would keep him cooling his jets outside on the porch a little longer.

"I'm trying to decide whether you're going to continue to give me a hard time or not. I've got a to-do list a mile long and it doesn't include arguing with you."

"I'm here to apologize. Not to argue."

She held the screen door open, then locked it behind him and headed to the coffeepot. "Apologize for what?"

"For putting you on the spot at the party on Saturday."

"I forgive you. Was there anything else?"

"Right." Reece chuckled. "Look, I am aware that you are keeping a list of all my misdeeds."

The expression on her face didn't refute his words.

"I apologize. I shouldn't have called you out in public. I was completely wrong."

Claire poured coffee into a mug. "Want some?"

"No, thanks."

She raised the mug to her lips and watched him over the rim.

Man, he'd like to know what was going on behind those blue eyes. While her expression gave away nothing, he had the distinct impression that he remained in the doghouse.

"All done. All done," Zoe sing-songed as she entered the kitchen. "Mr. Reece, we're going into the attic today."

"Oh, yeah? Looking for treasure?"

"No. A dollhouse. For me," Zoe said. "We're waiting for Miss Nan to come over to help us."

He met Claire's gaze. "Why don't you let me help you with that?"

"Yes, please," Zoe said.

"Sweetie, I think he was speaking to me," Claire said.

"But, Mommy, you said that Miss Nan was going to help you and now she's going to be late because she had to go help Mr. Asa."

"Is Asa all right?" Reece asked. He looked at Claire.

"He may have hurt his back. She's taking him into the clinic in town."

"Then let me help you in the attic."

"I don't know."

Zoe screwed up her face and tugged on her mother's arm. "Mommy, please."

"If you're sure," she said to Reece. "I know you're a very busy guy."

"Not too busy for my...for Zoe." He shot a

glance at Zoe. One of these days he was going to slip and say daughter and he wouldn't be remorseful. It was time to tell her and he was tired of waiting.

"Thank you, then." Claire put the mug on the counter and gave him the first smile of the day. "But let me warn you, I have no idea what to expect up there. My father rarely allowed me in the attic."

"Fair enough." He glanced down at her bare feet. "Shoes."

"Why?"

"You just said you don't know what's up there. Could be evidence of mice or a bat or broken glass on the ground."

Claire shivered and ran her hands up and down her arms. "Ugh. Good point." She slipped into her sneakers that were parked near the door. "There might be spiders. I don't do spiders, either."

"How about a flashlight so we can see the spiders before they see us?" he asked.

"Good idea." She rummaged in a drawer and pulled out two flashlights, testing both before handing one to Reece.

"Low ceiling?" Reece asked.

"Yes. My father had to stoop when he went in the attic."

Reece removed his hat and placed it on the doorknob.

"Can I come?" Zoe asked.

"No, ma'am. Not until we know if it's safe up there," Reece said. He stopped and looked at Claire, realizing he might be in trouble for overstepping again.

"Listen to Mr. Reece. Wait right here at the table and come and get me if someone comes to the door."

Reece said nothing about the tiny milestone that had just been reached when he spoke to Zoe like her parent. Claire hadn't challenged him. He tucked away a smile at the small victory as he followed Claire to the attic door on the second floor.

"You first," she said.

Reece raised a brow. "Because…"

"Because the last time I went in this attic, it gave me nightmares for weeks."

"How old were you?"

She put her fists on her hips. "Do not diminish my trauma. You go first."

Maintaining a straight face, he opened the door and climbed the few steps to a landing. Could it get any darker? "Is there a light switch around here?"

"On the wall. Hang on, I've got it."

The room lit up like a firefly streaking across a moonless night. He still could only see what his flashlight illuminated. "Why do attics always have bad lighting?" he muttered. "It's like a universal truth. June bugs come in spring and attic lightbulbs are all thirty-watt."

"To scare young children." The floorboards creaked when Claire stepped up to the landing and turned on her flashlight.

"Warm up here, too," he said. The air was thick and still with the lingering smell of mothballs and old newspapers.

"Yes. I'll need to open the vents and put a fan up here for the summer."

Reece walked to a small square window and cranked it open. "This one has a screen."

"Oh, that's better already," Claire said.

The ceiling proved to be as low as Claire remembered with a few unexpected hooks hanging at odd angles to hold plastic clothing-storage bags. The far right corner of the space held stacked furniture covered with moving blankets.

"Do you see your dollhouse?" Reece asked.

"No, but look over there."

Reece followed the beam of her flashlight to a pile of boxes stacked to the rafters. "What's that writing on the side?"

"They all say *Christmas*." Claire knelt down next to the boxes and pulled one out. She opened the lid and released a small gasp. "Ornaments," she murmured.

"You sound surprised."

"I am. I thought these were long gone."

"Long gone? What do you mean?"

"I mean the Ballards do not decorate."

"You didn't decorate for Christmas?"

"No. Nan gives the market a festive touch for customers. But that's it."

"Nothing in the house?"

"Not really."

"Your father was a church-going man. Didn't he celebrate the Lord's birth?"

"I suppose in his own way, but not at our house. Nan always invited us over for all the big holiday meals."

"What am I missing here?" he asked. "All these boxes of ornaments up here, yet your father didn't actually celebrate the holidays. I don't get it."

"He used to celebrate. A long time ago." Her voice was heavy with emotion as she examined the vintage glass ornament in her hand.

There was a story here, that much was clear. "Claire?"

"Hmm?" She looked up at him. The blue eyes seemed miles away.

"I'm here if you want to talk."

"Not today. But thank you." She put the ornament away, placed the lid on the box and slid it next to the others before she stood as if also pushing away the memories. "What does your family do for the holidays?" she asked.

"Not much until Tucker got married. Then his

wife had everyone over that first year. Last year, Daisy hosted Christmas dinner. That was pretty cool."

Claire dusted off her jeans and then jerked back. "What was that? Did you see something run across the floor?" She jumped, her elbow bumping his arm.

When Reece pivoted left, his head smacked into a wooden beam. "Whoa. Didn't see that coming."

"Oh, my. I am so sorry."

A moment later, a flashlight blinded him. "Claire, can you turn that off?"

"Oh, sorry, Reece. You hit your head."

"I know."

"You have a huge lump on your forehead."

"My fault for not looking both ways."

When her warm fingers touched his forehead, Reece froze, unable to breathe. Swallowing, he gently wrapped his fingers around her wrist and tugged her fingers away. "Claire, I'm fine."

"I'm a medical professional."

"I'm fine."

And even if he wasn't, the last thing he needed was Claire touching him.

Their eyes met in the dim light. "You don't look fine," she said softly, her gaze unwavering. "Are you sure?"

"It takes a lot more than that to take me out of

the game." His heart pounded in his chest at her genuine concern. Claire Ballard hadn't looked at him like that in six years.

He stepped away from her. A lifetime later and he still wasn't good enough for her, so he better not get used to her attention.

"If you say so," she said.

Flashlight leading the way, Reece scanned the attic. "Remind me what we're doing here and what we're looking for?"

"Terrific," she said. "Concussion and memory loss."

"I'm kidding, Claire."

"I know." She grinned like a kid. "So was I. See, I am not always literal."

Reece chuckled.

"Where would I be, if I were a dollhouse?" Peeking around an old bureau, Claire yanked off a furniture blanket and then coughed at the cloud of dust. "I found it," she sputtered.

He peered over her shoulder with his flashlight. "Claire, I was looking for a house for a doll. That thing is huge." The Victorian-style house stood over three feet high.

"My mother was a little extravagant. I asked for a house and got a mansion." She smiled with pride. "Look. The panels open and the windows open and close. It even has an attic."

"Wow. This sure beats the Barbie Dream

House hands down." He looked at her thinking about the pared-down lifestyle he came from. "You were an only child, so I suppose that's to be expected."

"Zoe's an only child," she said, voice indignant. "I don't overcompensate with material things."

"You know what? I'm just going to shut up." He moved around her and lifted the structure. "It's not heavy, but it sure is awkward. How about I take the front and you lift from the back?"

She tucked her flashlight in her pocket. "I'm ready."

"I'll go down the steps first. Slowly, or this house will land on me and that might take me out."

"Slow. Got it."

"One more step," Reece instructed.

Once they were out of the attic, the move to Zoe's room was easy.

"Zoe," Claire called. "Come on up here."

The five-year-old stood in the doorway for a moment, staring at the building before sliding to her knees. "Oh, Mommy, it's beautiful," she repeated over and over.

"It's dusty," Reece said.

"Zoe can dust it out." Claire knelt down next to her. "Get some rags from Grandpa's rag box and get started."

"Yes, Mommy."

"Are you ready for coffee?" Claire said to Reece.

"Yes, ma'am."

As they stepped into the kitchen, Nan's voice rang out. "Claire?"

"Nan, come on in."

"Door's locked."

"Oh, so sorry." Claire opened the screen.

"Reece, what happened to your head?" Nan's eyes rounded.

"Claire knocked me down."

"I did not."

Nan chuckled.

Claire stepped closer to Reece.

He stepped back.

"It looks worse. I'll get you an ice pack."

"Coffee is all I need right now. Mind if I help myself?"

"Go ahead," Claire said. She turned to Nan. "Do you know why there are so many boxes labeled *Christmas* in the attic?" Claire asked. "I thought my father got rid of everything that reminded him of Christmas years ago."

"He kept them?" Nan's voice registered surprise.

Claire nodded.

"I had no idea," Nan said.

"Someone want to explain why he didn't want to be reminded of Christmas?" Reece asked.

Nan looked at Claire as if waiting for her to respond.

"My mother left on Christmas Eve."

Reece could only stare for a moment, feeling her pain. He understood only too well what it was like to have a parent walk out of your life. "I'm really sorry."

"It was a long time ago."

Nan put an arm around Claire. "When you were little, younger than Zoe, your daddy used to decorate like crazy for the holidays. He'd even let the folks over at the Rebel nursery bring trees here to sell. Everyone came for miles to see Ballard Farm decorations. It used to be a big deal."

"I could barely get Dad to put up a Christmas tree when I was growing up."

"Maybe this is the year you change things up," Reece commented. He sipped the coffee and leaned against the counter thinking.

"I'm not going to be here in December."

Her words sliced right through him. "You don't know that," he said. "But that wasn't what I meant."

"Care to elaborate?"

"Christmas in July," he said.

"I bet a Christmas-in-July sale would bring in lots of tourists from Rebel Ranch for the peach picking," Nan added.

"Sure it would," Reece said. "July twenty-fifth.

Not much going on at the Ranch. Fourth of July has passed and the next big celebration is Labor Day."

"If you're going to go to that much trouble, you should have a party, too," Nan said. "What about a Christmas-in-July party here at the house?"

"Oh, I don't know." Claire scrunched up her face and grabbed her mug.

"Think about it," Reece said. "No Oklahoma ice storms. No chance of electricity going out. No windchill of minus ten."

Something inside of him said to keep pushing, even when she frowned.

"Maybe now is the time to create new memories." he added.

Claire's wide-eyed gaze shot to Nan.

"We were just talking about that," Nan said softly. "Replace old memories with new ones."

"See, Nan gets it. Making new memories for Zoe."

"For Zoe." Claire blinked, her eyes moist. "I guess it couldn't hurt."

"Claire, not hurting isn't the goal here," Reece said.

"Miss Nan, come up here and see my dollhouse."

"I'll leave you two to planning. I'm going up to see the dollhouse."

When Nan left the room, Claire cocked her

head and stared at him. "Why is it that despite all the knocks you've had in life, you remain so optimistic?"

"It's a choice, Claire."

Silence stretched.

"So what do you say?"

"Sure. Okay."

"That's the spirit. I like seeing you so enthusiastic."

She rolled her eyes. "What exactly do you have planned?"

Reece laughed. "No. I'm not planning this. We are."

"What do *we* have in mind?"

"The usual. Gift exchange. Dinner. Cheesy movies."

"I'll take care of the turkey and stuffing, and we'll invite our guests to bring the rest."

"Good plan." He stepped from the kitchen to the dining room "Pretty big room here. Does that table extend?"

"It does, though we never have."

"How many people do you suppose we could fit in here?" he asked.

"Not as many as you'd think. It will be crowded."

"Claire, that's the point. Crowd 'em all in, serve dinner buffet style."

She put her hand to her mouth in a familiar

gesture that said she was overwhelmed. "How many people do you have in mind?"

"Relax. Only family and close friends."

"Close friends?"

"Surely you have a few friends from Tulsa you can invite."

"One or two maybe."

"We're probably going to need two turkeys for twenty-some people."

"You cannot be serious. We will never fit twenty people in this house."

"This house is huge. We used to fit twenty in my mother's rinky-dink mobile home." He glanced around. "Don't worry. We got this."

"I'm way past worried. Now I'm concerned about the fire marshal shutting us down."

"Naw. It's going to be fun. You'll see."

"What about Ballard Farm?" she asked. "What sort of Christmas-in-July event will that entail?"

"I'm not sure, but I imagine Nan has some thoughts."

Nan stepped into the kitchen. "I nearly forgot how big that dollhouse is. It's a beauty, isn't it?"

"It is," Claire agreed. "Nan, I didn't even ask you about Asa."

"The doc wants us to take Asa up to Pawhuska for an MRI. His back is still bothering him and we want to get it done before the picking starts

Wednesday. That means I can't watch Zoe tomorrow."

"Oh, not a big deal. Asa comes first. I'll schedule Tulsa another time."

"Another time," Nan returned. "But tomorrow is your—"

Claire interrupted Nan with a nonverbal expression that said Reece had somehow missed a crucial piece of information in the conversation.

"Zoe can stay with me."

The room was silent for a moment. Reece spending time alone with his daughter. Was that enough to leave everyone speechless? He tamped back annoyance.

"Why, Reece, what a nice thing to offer," Nan said.

"You don't need to babysit Zoe," Claire said.

Reece frowned. "I don't think it's babysitting when it's your daughter."

"Reece," Claire sputtered as she looked at Nan, eyes round.

"Nan knows, and she knows I know she knows."

Nan started belly laughing, her shoulders shaking with mirth. "What he said."

"Are you sure you can handle Zoe for the day?" Claire asked. Her tone said she was not amused.

"You'd be surprised at what I can handle."

"Not me," Nan said. "I wouldn't be surprised."

Reece bit back a chuckle. Good to know he had both Asa and Nan rooting for him. He wasn't sure what exactly they were rooting for, but still, support was a good thing.

"Give me a chance, Claire," he said. "I watch my nieces and nephews all the time."

"Sure. Okay." The words came out slowly and thoughtfully. Whether it was Nan's influence or Claire had turned a corner of trust, he didn't know. Didn't care. He'd take what he could get and be happy.

"But no horses," she added.

"No horses."

"I'll make a list of contact phone numbers and important information."

"I wouldn't expect anything less."

"This is where I leave," Nan said. "I've got to get Asa lunch. I'll see you two later."

"Thanks, Nan," Claire said. "And tell Asa I'll be saying a prayer that his back feels better."

"I've got to get going, too," Reece said, when Nan left. He put his mug in the sink.

Claire nodded. "Thanks for your help with the dollhouse." She waved a hand in the air. "And I'm sorry about your head. Please put ice on it."

"I will and thank you, Claire. I know that wasn't an easy decision."

"Not easy, but you were right. It's not about Zoe. It's not even completely about you. It's about me."

"Maybe sometime we can talk about that."

"Sometime."

Reece headed to the truck. Sometime suddenly didn't seem like at no time. Maybe eventually they'd get to a place where she trusted him. Maybe even more than simply trusted him, though he wasn't sure what that meant. The only thing certain was that he had the summer to figure it all out, so he'd better hurry.

Chapter Six

Claire checked off a few more items on her lap-top to-do list while she nursed a handcrafted mocha latte on the patio of a popular T-town cof-feehouse. The Cherry Street district was abuzz with afternoon activity as shoppers and college students passed by on the sidewalk.

She finished off the chocolate croissant in front of her and relaxed, simply people watching for a few minutes. What an indulgent way to spend her birthday. How long had it been since she'd been out and about in the world without Zoe? A long time. Weeks ago, when her daughter had a playdate with a coworker's child.

Was it possible that a future with Reece in their life would yield some good changes along with the challenging ones?

Eyes on the laptop screen, she reviewed her list. Mail picked up at the post office and forwarding form completed online. *Check*. Zoe's toys packed up along with extra clothes for both of them. *Check*.

She'd met with her nursing supervisor, who again verbalized her displeasure at Claire's leave of absence, warning her that she couldn't promise to hold her position.

Claire rubbed a hand over her mouth. There was nothing she could do. The calendar reminded her that it was nearly July and she had a long time until her life was hers again. That was if everything went smoothly at the farm.

Looking back over the last three weeks, her life on Ballard Farm had actually found a rhythm. At sunrise, she'd let Blue out and then read her Bible. After breakfast, she and Zoe took Blue on a long walk to exercise the Lab. While Zoe had worked on her dollhouse, Claire attacked another part of her father's house. When Nan needed help, she and Zoe would offer assistance at the farm's market. Then, each night after dinner, she would read to Zoe before bed.

Claire had taken enough psychology courses to recognize that routines were her safety net. It was a day-by-day effort to put her trust in God instead of her schedule.

When an email popped up on her laptop, Claire eagerly opened it, recognizing the sender as a paper supply company. The holiday supplies she had ordered online had shipped and would be on her doorstep in three-to-five days. Another thing to check off her list.

Only twenty-four hours after Nan and Reece had come up with the Christmas-in-July idea, things were already moving. Claire was proud of herself for putting aside her fears and embracing the party idea.

She'd invited two of her favorite nurse friends, who were excited to drive out for the occasion and would spend the night at Rebel Ranch. Maybe Reece would spring for a friend-and-family discount at the guest ranch if she asked nicely.

Hosting her first party had her perfectionist tendencies working overtime. That meant yard work and cleaning the house. She found herself excited at the possibility that she would say goodbye to the bitter memories associated with Ballard Farm.

First, she had to get through the three days she'd committed to harvesting peaches.

Claire packed up her laptop and downed the rest of the beverage before heading to the car and then a gas station. After washing the windshield, she slid back into the car and checked her phone for messages. Nothing from Reece.

He'd looked at her like she was a grade-A helicopter mom when she'd given him a three-page list of phone numbers and information for Zoe, along with an indexed copy of her medical file.

When she insisted that he check in with her every hour, he had flat refused and said there was no point in her going to Tulsa if she wasn't going to cut the umbilical cord.

Was she being unreasonable? Didn't everyone provide that basic information? She'd confer with Daisy next time. The mother of seven could be counted on to be upfront with her. Claire tossed the phone into her purse.

No sooner had she put the phone down than it rang and she dug in the leather pouch to find it again.

Reece. She tensed and pressed the green button. When Zoe's smiling face appeared on the screen, relief was immediate.

"Zoe, honey. Are you all right?"

Her daughter giggled. "I lost a tooth, Mommy." She pointed to her top incisor, where a gap replaced one of her teeth.

"Oh, Zoe." A milestone for her only child and she'd missed it.

"Did it hurt when your tooth fell out?"

"Uh-uh." She shook her head. "I bit into my ice-cream cone and it came out. I laughed so hard. Mr. Willard taught me how to spit water through the space. I can do it almost as good as him."

"Is that right?" Claire smiled at the visual.

Zoe continued her breathless chatter. "Did you know Mr. Willard has three fingers on one of his hands? He does. A giant bear chased him and that's how he lost his fingers."

"That's quite a story."

Zoe grinned again. "When will you be home, Mommy?"

"Soon. I just got gas and I'm heading your way. About an hour."

"Yay. Mr. Reece says dinner will be ready in an hour."

"Dinner?" Claire paused at that information. "Sweetie, may I speak to Mr. Reece?"

"Mr. Reece, Mommy wants to talk to you." Zoe hollered out the request.

"Where is he?"

"He's chasing the cat."

"The cat?" Claire smiled at the thought of a big guy like Reece herding a cat.

"Mr. Reece has a naughty cat Mr. Tucker gave him. This morning he knocked all the pillows off the couch." Once again, her laughter rang out.

"Claire?"

Reece's face appeared on the screen and for a moment Claire was taken aback. Sometimes she forgot how handsome the man was. Today, his dark eyes sparkled with a hint of amusement and it was obvious he was happy. Happier than she'd ever seen him. Spending the day with his daughter had put that joy in his expression.

Claire worked to sort through this revelation.

"Hello? Can you hear me?"

"Yes. Yes. Sorry, Reece. Everything all right there?"

"Are you kidding? Everything is great."

"I'm glad." She tried to look past him to the background. "Where are you?"

"My house."

"Oh, I guess I thought you were at the ranch home."

"No. I have a perfectly good house." He paused and cocked his head. "You sound a little down. Tough day?"

Claire paused at his words. Did she ever imagine she'd be at a place in life where Reece Rainbolt asked her how her day was?

"No. It was actually a really good day. I guess I'm a little sad because Zoe lost her first tooth. Without me. Silly, I know."

"You can't plan those things, Claire. I'm sorry you missed it."

She was silent. Reece had missed a lot of firsts but he didn't remind her of that. He really was a much more magnanimous person than she gave him credit for. "Thank you for letting her call me."

"Sure. Just so you know, Zoe completed most of the chores on the list you provided."

"What else have you two been up to besides my list?"

"After lunch, I made an executive decision to play hooky, which is why she didn't finish all her chores."

"The list was a suggestion."

"Great, because we lost it, or it's possible the cat lost it. Willard and I took Zoe to town for an ice-cream cone and ran a few errands. Now we're making dinner." Another grin lit up his face, and a dimple appeared. "Zoe says she wants to be a chef when she grows up."

"She said that?" This was news to her.

"Yeah, about a dozen times. Hope you can stay for our amazing meat loaf."

"Oh, I don't know. I'm sure you have a lot to do. I've taken up most of your day already."

"No, you haven't. Zoe has, and I wouldn't have it any other way."

Zoe grabbed the phone. "Mommy, Mr. Reece and Mr. Willard took me with them to town to buy supplies."

"I heard about that."

"And they bought wood to make tree swings for the backyard. They said I should have swings so that other kids can come over and play. Can other kids come over and play?"

When Claire didn't immediately answer, Zoe charged ahead. "Please, Mommy."

"Yes. Yes. We can invite them over."

"Thank you, Mommy."

"I better hang up, Zoe, so I can get back to Rebel."

"For meat loaf," Zoe said. "You have to stay for meat loaf."

"Meat loaf. Got it."

Claire did her best to focus on the road and not Reece or Zoe or that she'd missed a major milestone in her daughter's life. She started an audiobook and then stopped it when she realized she was well into chapter four and hadn't heard a single word.

US Highway 412 proved to be a quiet drive home on a Tuesday afternoon. Home. When did Ballard Farm become home again?

Claire glanced out the window at the abandoned oil wells dotting the scenery. On a hill in the distance, cattle grazed in the sun. She'd always liked this drive, but in the past she had appreciated it more when she headed back to Tulsa and her life there.

As she took a turn in the road past the town of Prue, a Rebel, Oklahoma, sign appeared. Ten miles. She could go straight to Reece's. Claire glanced over her shoulder at the back seat. Except there was no room for Zoe unless she stopped home first to empty the car of boxes.

And quickly. Suddenly it seemed like she'd

been away from her daughter for days instead of hours.

Nan stood in the drive next to the Ballard Ranch pickup truck when Claire pulled in. She waved a greeting to Claire. "I signed for a letter for you. Looks important."

"Thanks." Claire jumped out of the car.

"You in a hurry?" Nan asked.

"I have to pick up Zoe." Claire smiled. "I haven't seen her all day."

"Ah, that's right. Asa and I stopped in town to fill his prescription and ran into Reece, Zoe and Willard at the Arrowhead Diner. Your daughter was having a great time."

"So I hear." A great time without her.

Claire took the letter and examined the envelope, assessing the official City of Rebel stationary. "This is from the mayor." She slid her finger beneath the flap, tore open the envelope and pulled out the stationary.

"It is?" Nan edged closer to read over Claire's shoulder.

"The town council voted to name the community center after my father." Claire stared at the paper for a moment, stunned and speechless. "I… don't know what to say."

"Oh, Claire, that's so wonderful."

"They're having a ceremony in August."

"Isn't that something? And so well deserved."

Claire turned to Nan. "You'll tell Asa?"

"Yes. Absolutely."

In a heartbeat, Claire came back to earth. "How is he?"

"Hard to tell since I can barely get him to tell me when he's hurting. Considers it a sign of weakness," Nan scoffed. "All I know is that he'll be in the orchards tomorrow and the day after that and the day after that, until the doc says no." She glanced at her watch. "I better scoot. I'm off to pick up groceries for tomorrow. I'm cooking for the pickin' crew."

"I don't know how you do it all. In fact, I am starting to realize I underestimated how much work you, Asa and my father put into this farm."

"It's a calling all right."

"Yes," Claire agreed.

"When we have a little more time, I want to talk to you about some ideas I have for the Christmas-in-July sale. For the market."

"How long have you run the market, Nan?"

Nan frowned in thought. "Your father hired us thirty years ago. You were three years old."

"After thirty years, I think you know what you're doing. Whatever you want to do with the market, you have my carte blanche approval."

"Aw, thanks. But what about Reece?"

"I'm sure he'd agree, but the fact is, the market is on my side of the inheritance." She winked and turned to open the trunk.

"Oh, and, Claire, I left a little something for you on your back porch."

Claire raised a brow.

"Did you think I would forget it was your birthday?"

She reached out to hug the older woman. "You never have."

"Shame it always falls right in the middle of harvest."

"After all these years, I'm used to postponing it until my dad had time."

By the time Nan had driven the pickup down the drive, Claire had brought the plants from the back seat into the house.

On her way back to the car she stepped off the porch and blinked when she realized that Baby stood in the yard, staring at her. "Baby? What are you doing here?"

"I'm guessing she likes your grass better than ours."

Claire whirled around to see Willard awkwardly hop over the fence.

"You must be Mr. Cornell."

"We haven't had the pleasure." He pulled off his gloves and Claire noted that Zoe was right. He had three fingers on one of his hands.

"Don't mind my missing fingers. I lost them to a bobcat in a wrestling match."

Claire's lips twitched.

"Nice to meet you, Mr. Cornell."

"Willard will do." He gave a solemn nod. "I'm sorry for your loss, ma'am. Davis Ballard was a fine man."

"Thank you for that." She looked over at the cow. "How did you know Baby was here?"

"I didn't. I was checking the fences and found one down. Figured she leaned against it. The wood is so old, it just fell over." He shrugged. "I followed her prints in the grass."

"Smart cow." She reached for another box from the back seat.

"You want some help with those?"

"That would be great. I'm running late to pick up Zoe and I have half a dozen more in the trunk."

"Nice little girl you got there. Looks a lot like her daddy."

"Excuse me?" Claire slowly turned around.

"For what?"

"You said she looks like Reece."

"I said she looks like her daddy." He offered a smile. "Hasn't anyone ever mentioned that?"

Claire paused, realizing that if he had any doubts, she'd just confirmed it. There was no turning back now. "How did you know? I mean about Reece being her father?"

"Aw, I put my boot in mouth again, didn't I?" He shook his head. "That seems to be my favorite pastime of late. I'm sure sorry, ma'am."

"No, not at all, but how? How did you know?"

"I got eyes." He shrugged and adjusted the brim of his cowboy hat. "If it's any consolation, I haven't said anything to anyone 'cause I thought it was common knowledge."

"I guess it's about to be." Shame tried to smother her, but Claire slapped it away.

What had she expected? Secrets always turned out badly in the end and she knew that better than anyone.

"Reece Rainbolt has a little girl. Around these parts that's what we call good news." He grabbed two boxes. "Where do you want these?"

"Just stack them in the kitchen."

Willard made several trips to the house and finished unloading the trunk before she had the back seat emptied.

"You're fast," Claire said.

He laughed. "Been called a lot of things. Fast is not one of them. At my age, I'm only two steps ahead of Baby on a good day." He nodded toward the dining room, where Blue whined and pawed at the door. "You want me to take the dog for a walk while I'm at it?"

"Oh, Willard. Would you? I've been gone all day, and he hasn't been out since Reece took him this morning."

"No problem."

"Just lock the screen door behind you?" She smiled with gratitude. "I've got a couple of peach loaves on the counter in foil. Grab one for yourself."

His eyes lit up. "Now you're talking my language. Thank you."

"You're welcome and thank you." Claire headed out the door.

"Ms. Ballard?"

She turned back. "Call me Claire."

"You're the boss, and where I come from, we don't take familiar with the boss."

"Fair enough. Did you have a question?"

"No, ma'am. But you forgot this." He picked up a gaily wrapped package with *happy birthday* scrawled on the attached card. "Found it behind your flowerpot."

"Oh, thank you."

"And happy birthday." He nodded toward the present.

"Thank you for that, too." She opened the car door. "Can you tell me which house is Reece's?"

"Drive past the main house and take a left before you get to the cabins. Keep going. First house is Tucker's and the second one is Reece's."

The second house was much larger than Tucker's modest ranch home. In fact, Reece's house looked like some sort of lodge. Two stories with three chimneys and lots of stone and rough-hewn wood. Claire nearly drove right past it. She slammed on the breaks, tossing the mail to the floor.

No. Surely, this wasn't Reece's house. Claire pulled into the drive and got out of the car. What did he do with all that space? Who cleaned it?

When Zoe came running out the front door toward her, arms outstretched, Claire realized she was wrong. This absolutely was Reece's house. She picked up her sagging jaw in time to see Reece following behind, hands tucked in his pockets.

"I missed you, my little girl." Claire grabbed Zoe in a bear hug.

"See, she's all in one piece," Reece said. "Well, except for the tooth."

Zoe grinned and offered her face for inspection. Claire got down on her knees and looked. "That's amazing." When Zoe wrinkled her nose, Claire brushed white powder from it.

"Flour," Reece said.

Claire straightened and assessed Reece as he stood against the backdrop of his home. His navy T-shirt had a sprinkling of flour on the pocket and she bit back a chuckle.

Like father, like daughter. The thought came unbidden to her mind. And she realized that wasn't such a bad thing.

"What's so funny?" he asked.

"You have flour on your shirt."

He glanced down and brushed at his shirt until it disappeared. "Are you going to come on in?"

Claire shook her head and once again glanced up at his house. "That's quite a man cave, Reece," she said.

"Try not to sound so surprised."

"Who cleans a place this size?"

He laughed. "I hire someone."

"I'm a little stunned. Why such a big house?"

"Because I dream big, Claire. I always have." A broad smile reached to his eyes, the effect creating havoc with her heart.

"I guess so," she murmured.

"Are you staying for dinner?" he asked.

"Please, Mommy."

"Dinner." She looked from Reece to Zoe and knew that refusal was not an option. "Sure. If I get a tour of the house."

"We can do that. Right, Zoe?"

"Right."

Claire remained in silent awe as Reece walked her through his home—a home that was easily camera ready for a layout in *Architectural Digest*. Was the minimalist decor with hints of south-west flair his style or the decorator's? Either way, Claire liked it a lot.

"The kitchen is this way," Reece said with a grimace. "Excuse the mess, we've been working."

She stepped into a huge modern kitchen in oak and granite. And stopped. Countertops were filled with used mixing bowls and measuring cups. Flour had been dusted across every surface. "I.... What happened?"

"We made a cake," Zoe burst out. "It's a surprise."

Reece nodded toward their daughter. "She told me it's your birthday today."

"Zoe, how did you remember my birthday?"

"Miss Nan told me. We made a beautiful cake, Mommy."

"Let's eat first," Reece said.

Minutes later, the three of them sat at the huge dining room table. Zoe's chair was stacked with books so she could reach her meal.

"This is delicious," Claire admitted. "I never liked meat loaf before today. I don't even make meat loaf."

"I watch that Oklahoma television chef who lives up in Pawhuska. That woman brings home the goods. All her recipes are on the money."

She stared at him. "You watch cooking shows?"

"A man has to eat." He placed his silverware on his plate. "You cook, right?"

"Yes. Nan taught me."

"Mitch taught me. Someone had to feed the family when Mitch was working. We all took turns."

When Zoe tugged on her sleeve, Claire turned. "Yes, sweetie?"

"Are you done, Mommy? Because we have another big, big surprise."

"Okay. Let me clear these plates before the surprise."

"No way. You're the guest and it's your birthday. I got this." Reece turned to Zoe. "Zee, can you get the special thing?"

Zee? He called her Zee? Eight hours and he had a nickname for his daughter.

Zoe nodded, her little shoulders quivering with excitement.

"Claire, you have to close your eyes," Reece said.

She complied and heard giggles and a clatter of dishes. When Reece brushed against her arm, she smelled chocolate. Rich chocolate fudge.

"Open your eyes."

"Surprise!" Zoe called out.

Reece slid a chocolate cake in front of her. Claire stared at the layer cake. Sure, it was a bit lopsided, but Zoe and Reece had made that cake. She'd never seen anything more beautiful. A sweet ache touched her heart.

"Happy birthday!" Zoe held out a flat box with a lopsided bow. "Open it, Mommy. Open it."

Claire unwrapped the box and carefully removed the lid. Inside was a beautiful polished brass picture frame with a photo of a smiling Zoe with her missing tooth evident.

Claire looked up at Reece. "This is precious. How did you do this?"

"There's a photo printer at the ranch. We picked out the frame in town. I mean, Zoe picked it out."

"It's beautiful. Thank you so much." She snagged her daughter around the waist for a hug, and then she looked to Reece, emotion barely restrained. This was the most thoughtful gift she'd ever received. Claire rose and hesitantly faced the tall cowboy.

Reece stood very still, his gaze unwavering and his eyes warm with something she didn't recognize as she reached out and hugged him. For a moment, she savored the embrace, foolishly thinking about how things might have been.

"Thank you," Claire said. "This is the best birthday ever."

"You haven't tasted our cake yet," he said softly, his gaze lingering on her face.

"My review stands. Best birthday ever. However, I am ready for cake. What kind is it?"

"Your favorite, Mommy."

"Chocolate fudge with chocolate frosting."

"Oh, my." Claire sat down and scooped up a bit of frosting with her finger and tasted it. "Is this from scratch?" she asked, marveling at the flavor.

"We don't use box mixes in this restaurant," Reece returned.

"It's delicious," Claire said.

Reece held up his palms. "High five, Chef Zee. You're awesome."

Claire sat mesmerized as the three of them laughed together. This was all kinds of wonderful. Sort of their private little world.

But what would happen when the outside world intruded and found out Zoe was Reece's daughter and Claire didn't plan to stay in Rebel? That she intended to take her away from all this come August.

She glanced around the dining room, her gaze spanning the tall windows and the stunning view that looked out on acres and acres of Rebel Ranch.

In a heartbeat, a startling thought hit her. Why would Zoe want to live in Tulsa in their little apartment, when she could have all this? And who was she to deny her daughter everything Reece could give her?

Her stomach knotted as question after question attacked without a single answer.

"Another cup of coffee?" Reece asked.

Claire held up a hand. "I'm good. Completely

full, but good." She glanced at her watch. "We have to get going. Peach harvest starts tomorrow." His gaze followed hers to the living room where Zoe had fallen asleep on the couch with Tucker's cat at her side.

"Before I forget." Reece pulled a small plastic bag from his jeans pocket. "For the under the pillow thing."

"Under the pillow thing?"

The moment Claire crossed her arms, a speeding *uh-oh* shot through his mind. Reece placed the coffee carafe on the table and sat down. "Is that a problem?"

"That practice? Well, it's not exactly reality, Reece. I don't do that sort of thing with Zoe."

"Reality? Reality is a little kid living in a sad trailer park with a sick momma and no daddy. Too many bills and not enough food. I've had my fill of reality." He released a slow breath and folded his hands together. "You let her watch movies about princesses and knights in shining armor. Where's the reality in that?"

"We discuss the movies and what's real and what is fiction."

"Seriously, Claire? Do her eyes glaze over?"

Claire didn't answer. She picked up her cup and sipped as though carefully sorting through several distasteful options for an appropriate response.

Okay, points for patience, he conceded.

"I think it's important to be honest and not create false realities," she finally said.

Reece nearly bit off his tongue trying not to knee jerk in response. "How does not telling her I'm her father fit into that theory?"

"Are you making fun of me?"

"Not you. But yeah, I guess I am poking fun at the entire situation."

"Willard knows about Zoe."

"He does? Who told him?"

"He's got good eyes."

Reece chuckled. "That's laughable since Willard has selective vision and hearing."

"You're taking all of this very lightly," Claire said.

She'd gone from relaxed to tense faster than he'd expected. And he found his annoyance threshold edging toward the red zone.

"Maybe you could tell me how you want me to take this, Claire. Zoe is my daughter and if Willard knows, then soon enough my family and other friends will realize that I'm her father, too." He shrugged. "I'm willing to deal with the fallout, but I want to be the one who delivers this particular news."

"People will talk and this is a small town. You may be willing to deal with the fallout but I'm not."

"That's what you're afraid of?" Reece shook

his head. "Here's a news flash. You and I aren't perfect. We both have fallen short. But thanks to God's mercy we get a do-over. I am grateful for a second chance. I asked for His forgiveness and yours. Now I'll get a chance to ask for Zoe's."

He raised his palms. "From this point on, it's all good as far as I can tell."

Claire stared at him, surprised. Well, she wanted reality. This was reality.

"What do you suggest we do next?" she asked.

"I suggest we tell Zoe before someone else does."

Claire bit her lip. "When?"

"The sooner the better."

"Could you come over next Sunday for dinner?"

"The weekend after the Fourth of July? Sure. I can do that."

"Maybe we should have a game plan. A script." She nodded and he could see Claire's planning and organizing wheels turning in her head—a sure sign of trouble ahead.

"You said five-year-olds want simple explanations," he said.

"Yes. That's true, but this is different. It seems as though we should be prepared. We're co-parenting now. We should have a united front."

"Co-parenting. Isn't that a fancy word? We're

her parents, Claire. How about if we relax and turn it over to God?"

"That seems a little…"

"Unscripted?"

"Unprepared."

He fully expected her to pull out a pen and paper and start making a list.

"Reece?" she prompted when he didn't answer. "I think we should talk about how we're going to handle people's responses. Don't you?"

"People's responses are going to be happy. That's it."

They were both silent for moments. Reece almost…almost regretted his outburst a few minutes ago. Except that it needed to be said. Today was one of the best days of his life, because he'd spent it with his daughter. Zoe was a Rainbolt. He wanted the world to know, and he wanted more days like today.

"Ever think about staying in Rebel?" he asked.

"What?" Claire blinked, confusion in her eyes.

"They have a medical clinic here in Rebel."

She fiddled with the rim of her coffee cup. "I don't know. My job in Tulsa…"

"Is a paycheck the only thing that's keeping you tied to T-town?"

Claire met his gaze. "Reece, I can't go there right now. I'm torn between two worlds. My father's and mine."

"Maybe you need to consider Zoe's world."

She jerked back. "That's not fair."

"I'm not trying to be argumentative. But you've told me your father put the farm first instead of his child. What would putting you first look like? What does putting Zoe first look like?"

Claire opened her mouth and closed it without answering. "You're asking me the same questions that I wrestle with in the middle of the night. I don't have an answer yet."

"I get that. I really do. But do you want Zoe ping-ponging between Tulsa and Rebel for the next thirteen years? Summers away from you. Holidays with me?"

"I honestly hadn't thought that far ahead."

"Maybe you should. Zoe starts school soon, and we'll have to make some custody decisions."

"I know, but I tend to work in a linear manner and right now I'm dealing with today's worries. Oh! I almost forgot. I have something." She reached for her purse and pulled out a letter. "This came today."

Reece skimmed the letter. "The Davis Ballard Community Center. Claire, this is quite an honor. You should be proud of your father. And this is something that Zoe can share with her children."

Claire stared at him. "I hadn't thought of it like that."

"Family. Heritage. Ancestry. It means a lot. It's

what defines our identity and unites us. It's what kept the Rainbolt kids together in hard times."

"I have to admit, you make me think beyond today to the bigger picture. It's a good thing, even if it is scary." She paused. "Will you come to the ceremony with us?"

"Absolutely. This is your father's legacy and I want to be a part of the moment." Reece looked from the letter to Claire one more time. "I believe we have a responsibility to teach Zoe to honor her heritage." He paused. "It's your heritage, too, Claire. Don't throw it away because you're afraid."

Chapter Seven

"I have never been so tired in my life." Claire pulled off her straw hat and pushed back matted strands of hair that had escaped from her ponytail. A river of sweat trickled down her face and she wiped it away. Lunch was nearly over and the combination of carbs and exhaustion had turned her limbs to jelly and made her want to crawl under the table for a nap.

"Being a nurse is hard work," Reece said.

"Let me rephrase that. I've never been so tired, hot, sticky and sore in my entire life." She slapped at a bug that landed on her arm. "This is much more physically straining than nursing. I'm up and down the ladders because I'm too short to pick the high branches and too tall for the short ones. So basically this is a free step class without the gym membership."

"Yeah, and it's a hot one today. The peach juice

I've got all over me isn't helping the mosquito-and-fruit-fly situation, either."

"I feel like such a slacker," Claire continued. "I did this all summer when I was younger. If I was getting a quarter a bushel today, I'd barely have enough money to fill my gas tank."

"The keyword here is younger."

"Still, I could never be a farmer like my father. I'm a wimp."

He laughed. "You are not a wimp."

"How do you do it?" she asked him. "You run Rebel Ranch and you're hands-on. Plus, you're much older than me."

"I'm only four years older." He stared at her unamused.

Claire chuckled.

"The secret is that I do it every day. If you worked the farm every day, you'd be physically prepared."

She doubted she'd ever be in the kind of physical shape he was in. Claire raised her head and looked at him. Really looked at him. Reece was a contradiction. She'd seen him in a suit in the attorney's office, where he was every inch the businessman entrepreneur, but out here, the man was in his element, all broad shoulders and larger than life.

He was correct when he said that she didn't know him. After her visit to his home last night and seeing him with Zoe, she realized that she was only just beginning to peel the onion on this new Reece Rainbolt. Claire found herself intrigued and attracted to the man he'd become.

Being attracted to Reece was a terrible idea if she wanted life to return to the way it was. And she did. Didn't she? Every day, the line between the past and the present blurred a little bit more and the fence around her heart seemed ready to topple.

Claire groaned and rubbed a hand over her face.

"It's not that bad, Claire. You own the farm."

"Half of the farm."

"Half of the farm. And there is a certain amount of management that goes into that. If you hire the right people, there's less micromanagement going on."

"My father already did that. Asa and Nan."

"That's not enough. Asa and Nan have been running circles around you and me for years, but they're getting older. Did you see Asa? You're a nurse. He didn't look too good."

Claire nodded. Though he tried to hide it, Asa's color was off and the usually robust farmer seemed wan.

"I've been really assessing the operation and I have concerns, Claire."

"You said the place needs a refresh. I get that."

She looked around and already the evidence of Willard's hard work could be seen. The fences had been repaired and the market building had a new coat of paint.

"More than that," Reece said. "Nan manages the market and yet she's out mowing the lawn in the orchard." He shook his head. "I see examples of that over and over. The staff is spread too thin."

"Can we afford to hire more staff?"

"We can't afford not to. There's an initial up-front hit, but increasing staff will increase production and there will be less fruit ripening before it can be picked. That means increased income."

"I heard that, and I am all for it." Nan approached with plates of brownies for the picking crew.

"Good, because I'm bringing in some of my men from the ranch tomorrow."

"Isn't this your busiest time of year?" Claire protested.

"It is but I've got an entire part-time crew of college kids who work summers who would love the hours until classes start in August. They'll work the orchards and help Willard spruce this place up for your Christmas-in-July sale, too."

"You're always a step ahead of me, Reece." It was Claire's turn to shake her head. "You should be running Ballard Farm. I'm not much help."

"Not true. You're a Ballard. It's in your blood."

She offered a weak smile. "I appreciate the pep talk but somehow I don't see myself walking in my father's shoes anytime soon." And she wasn't convinced she wanted to.

Reece reached for a brownie. "Thank you, Nan."

Claire glanced around. Her daughter was usually first in line for brownies. "Where's Zoe?"

"She's asleep on the hammock," Nan said. "I'll run her up to the house for her nap in a few minutes, so those skeeters don't get her."

"Thank you for keeping her while we pick. I know that makes double duty for you. Or triple, as Reece just pointed out."

"Nah, no big deal. I did it when you were little."

"Yes. You did."

"Nan, how's Asa holding up?" Reece asked.

"I'm guessing that once I tell him you're bringing more help in tomorrow, he'll be much better."

"Any word on his MRI?" Claire asked.

"Holiday tomorrow. The doctor's office is closed today, but we have an appointment for a follow-up next week."

"What do the pick-your-own appointments look like for Saturday?" Reece asked.

"We're booked from seven a.m. to near dark tomorrow. We'll cut off early due to the fireworks over at Rebel Lake. Still, the Fourth of July is going to be a long day."

"Wait a minute. Did you say appointments?" Claire asked. "When did you start taking appointments?"

"This year," Nan said. "It was Reece's idea. He even put an ad in the *Weekly Rebel*."

Claire blinked. "That's genius."

"It will help with staffing and lets us know what to expect in terms of sales," Nan said.

"I've got Violet at the ranch working on a web page so they can be automatically booked," Reece said.

"That's great, too," Claire said. "Will we turn down walk-ins?"

"Never turn down a sale," Reece said.

Claire nodded and turned to Nan. "Is the market open the entire holiday weekend?"

"Tomorrow for the Fourth of July and only in the afternoon on Sunday."

"I'll help," Claire said. "I can man the cash register."

"Take Zoe to the parade first," Nan said. "She's never seen the parade, has she?"

"Nan, you going to bring those brownies over here," someone hollered, "or you gonna let Rainbolt eat them all?"

Reece laughed and grabbed another brownie before Nan left to share the treats.

"So Zoe's never been to the parade, huh?"

"Um, no," she murmured. Zoe hadn't ever seen the parade because, in past years, Claire had stayed away from downtown Rebel to avoid running into Reece.

"Mind if I catch up with you two downtown tomorrow?" he asked.

"Zoe would like that."

"Great." Reece nodded and glanced at his watch. "Only a few more hours and we're free."

"A few more hours? Sunset isn't until quarter to nine."

"I'm trying to put positive spin on things," he said.

"Nice try." Claire smiled. "You know this whole farming thing wouldn't be so bad if it was nine to five with the weekends off."

"Yeah, but then it wouldn't be called farming. It would be called dreaming."

"Okay, you got me there."

"The thing is you work harder than you ever have in your life during the summer and make enough money to sustain the business in the slow winter months. It's a trade-off."

"Is the ranch open all year round?" Claire asked.

"We are, though things are scaled back significantly on the guest side, so we've added some revenue streams to increase our income during off-season."

"Really? Like what?"

"We built a chapel with a gazebo and a reception hall. It's used for wedding venues and family reunions. Sometimes for photography sessions. It's been really popular. Spring and fall are the busiest months. I had to hire someone to handle that side of the business."

"Wow," she breathed. "You're really good at this, aren't you?"

"Again, you're surprised." He gave a slow shake of his head.

"You're right. I do underestimate you. Apparently, everything I've heard about you since I arrived is true."

Reece narrowed his eyes. "Could you elaborate?"

She gave him a laughing smile as she stood. "I'd love to, but lunch break is almost over and I'm going to run Zoe to the house for Nan. I don't want her to have to carry her all that way."

"Let me do it,"

Claire opened her mouth to refuse and stopped. "Okay, sure. Thank you."

"That wasn't so hard, was it?" Reece said.

"What do you mean?"

"Giving me a chance." He stood and grinned.

"And correct me if I'm wrong, but I think we may have just co-parented without a script."

Claire smiled at his retreating form. It was hard to refute him when he was right and he was so cute.

She grabbed the bottle of insect repellant from the table and rubbed it on her exposed skin as she mentally prepared for the afternoon. It was a little after 1:00 p.m. All she had to do was make it until sunset and she was done. Claire picked up her water bottle and gloves. Eight more hours. That was all. She palmed her forehead at the thought.

When thirty minutes passed without a sign of Reece, she peered through the branches of trees for him. Usually, they picked near each other and discussed the peach production. This morning it was a long conversation on high-tech solutions for bird control in the orchard versus propane cannons that would terrify the cattle and horses on Rebel Ranch.

"Maybe he's helping Nan," she murmured aloud.

"Claire."

The urgency in Reece's voice had Claire spinning around so fast her balance on the ladder teetered.

"Whoa." Reece's hands caught her around the waist and lifted her to ground.

She stepped back from the warmth of his touch. "What's wrong?"

"Zoe's looking a little punk. I'm no expert but she feels warm to me, too." Concern filled his eyes. "I think you should be with her."

Claire pulled off her picking apron and handed it to him.

"Would it be all right if I come by and check how she's doing when I'm done here?"

"Yes. Sure." She paused and put a hand on his arm. "Thank you, Reece."

By the time Claire got to the house, Zoe was asleep again. She had fallen asleep with her hands tucked under her pillow. Claire put a hand to her forehead. Reece was right. She was warm.

Zoe shifted in the bed, her eyes fluttered open and then closed.

"I love you, Mommy."

"I love you, too, baby."

The bedside table held a glass of water and a washcloth. Claire smiled. Reece must have done that.

As her daughter drifted back to sleep, Claire said a silent prayer for health and offered a thanks to God for the blessings of a child in her life.

The sun had set by the time Reece appeared at the back door. Claire had showered, given Zoe a bath and put her back to bed.

"Come in, Reece," she said.

"How's she doing?"

"Low-grade fever, but it broke and she had some broth and crackers. She's fine."

"What causes that?"

"Fever of unknown origin. Who knows?" Claire shrugged. "There have been a lot of people in and out of the farm. She probably picked something up. The good news is it passed quickly."

"May I peek in on her?"

"Sure. Do you remember which room is hers?"

"Maybe you better show me. It's dark up there and I don't want to bang into something and wake her."

"Come on."

"You go first," he said. "I haven't showered and you have. Your nose won't be happy if I go first."

She laughed. "You've got the wrong girl if you think I've got a sensitive nose. I'm knee-deep in all sorts of challenging scents at the hospital."

"Just the same. My pride could use a break."

He silently followed her up the stairs. Claire pointed to Zoe's door. It was cracked open and a night-light illuminated her bed as she slept.

Reece stood at the door for long minutes, watching her sleep. "I don't know how you do it," he whispered.

"Do what?"

"Handle when she gets sick. I almost had a meltdown. My heart was in my throat and I couldn't breathe when I realized she had a fever. Thought I was going to pass out."

"I'm a nurse and I have medical training. Think about Daisy. She's a rookie mother with seven kids. That woman deserves a medal."

"Rookie is right. Her grandmother raised her. Did you know that?"

"No."

He nodded toward the stairs and they returned to the kitchen. Reece slid into a chair at the kitchen table.

"Yep. They're real close. She comes in the summer from Arizona and helps Daisy out."

"Coffee?" Claire asked.

"That'd be great."

She turned, opened the cupboard, pulled out two mugs and put them on the table. "What about your family, Reece? You always talk around your past, but I gather your brother Mitch raised you and your younger siblings. That had to be tough, too."

"I thought you knew? I thought everyone in Rebel knew about those poor Rainbolt kids."

She stared at him. "I have no clue what you're talking about. I only know bits and pieces of what you've mentioned. About your mom passing and inheriting the land and you cooking for the family while Mitch was supporting everyone." She paused. "You never talked much about yourself… even when I knew you in Tulsa."

Warmth rushed up her neck and she glanced away. "Back then, you talked about the rodeo and that was pretty much all."

"Isn't that funny? Or maybe just pathetic. All my life I've figured that you heard all the town rumors about the Rainbolts and that's why you never talked much to me in high school. I mean you were so out of my league. You got off the bus at the big house at Ballard Farm. I was end of the line at the trailer court."

She stared at him for a moment processing the admission. He thought she was out of his league?

"Reece, I never talked much to you because I was shy and you were a pretty big man on campus. In those days, I didn't talk to anyone. I escaped life by reading." She shook her head. "Besides, if I got off at the first stop and you got off at the last, how would I know where you lived?"

"Huh. Go figure."

Claire filled the carafe with water and poured it into the reservoir as Reece's words circled through her.

"Reece, can I ask you a question?"

"Hmm?"

"Why did you dump me?"

The room was silent, except for the hum of the refrigerator. Finally, Claire turned around.

Reece sat at the table with his head propped on his hand, sound asleep. For a few minutes, she stared at his profile and watched the steady rise and fall of his chest. There were so many conflicting thoughts when it came to her daughter's father.

She prided herself on her good sense, yet when she looked at him, it sailed right out the door and her heart screamed to trust him.

Things were about to get even more complicated on Sunday when they told Zoe that Reece was her father.

Claire sighed and turned off the coffeepot. Now she'd have to wake him up and send him along home. Good thing he only lived next door.

"Mommy, I want a daddy like Mr. Reece. How can we do that?"

"What?" Claire fumbled with the glass in her hand. As if in slow motion, it slipped from her fingers, bounced against her knee and then kissed the kitchen floor, crashing into tiny pieces.

Both Claire and Zoe stared at the floor in stunned surprise.

"You broke it, Mommy." She began to hop down from her chair at the kitchen table.

"No! Zoe! Stop!"

Zoe's eyes rounded and she froze.

"That can cut you. Never pick up broken glass. Stay where you are. I'll sweep it up."

Claire grabbed the broom and dustpan and quickly cleaned up the shards. "Now stay still. I'm going to wipe down the floor to make sure there aren't any loose pieces."

"Mr. Reece says it's okay to make messes."

"Does he?"

"Uh-huh. He says having fun is as important as hard work."

"Great. But if I don't clean this up really well, then Blue might cut himself." She dragged the mop back and forth in neat lines, carefully rinsing it in the sink between swipes.

"So, um, Zoe. What made you think about Mr. Reece today?"

"I colored a picture of a family in my coloring book." She lifted the book up for Claire to look. "See. A mommy. A daddy. A little boy and girl, and a dog."

"Zoe, you know that there are all kinds of families."

"Uh-huh. But Mr. Reece doesn't have a little girl or a little boy and he likes me and I like him. Mr. Reece says family is very important." With that last bit of information, Zoe hopped off her chair and strode down the hall to the restroom.

When had Reece become the designated adult

in her family? He had her daughter quoting random pearls of wisdom. Last Saturday, at the Fourth of July parade, it had been the same thing.

Mr. Reece says. Mr. Reece says. Finally, against her better judgment, Claire had bought Zoe cotton candy to distract her.

When Reece joined them at the parade, he lifted Zoe high on his shoulders to watch and she was thrilled. Granted, it was nice to be a sort of family unit among all the families at the parade, but most of the time, Zoe forgot all about her mother as she beamed under the adoring eyes of the rancher next door.

This morning had been a repeat of the same at Sam's birthday party yesterday. The two of them had participated in every party game. Reece played pin-the-tail-on-the-Brahma-bull. The two were BFFs to the point where Tucker, Mitch and Daisy exchanged knowing glances.

She couldn't blame them. With their heads close together, Zoe and Reece were clearly lookalikes with their dark hair and matching eyes. The upside was that it was just as Reece predicted—no big deal—when he officially told his family.

Logically, she understood the process. Reece had mentally given birth to a five-year-old girl. He was in the honeymoon stage. He'd never seen a mindboggling ten-minute tantrum when Zoe refused to wear boots when it was snowing or accidentally flushed a doll head down the toilet resulting in a two-hundred-dollar plumber visit.

It was all sunshine and lollipops right now.

She didn't begrudge him his joy. Not a bit.

While the sight of Zoe and Reece bonding warmed Claire, it worried her at the same time. Her daughter was falling in love with Reece, and the more he became a daddy, the more Claire let her guard down. All in the name of Zoe's happiness.

Claire feared that the more time she spent with Reece, the closer she was to finding herself near the edge of a precipice. All it would take to have her tumbling down the hill to disaster and falling in love with the cowboy once more was a little nudge. She couldn't do it again. The last time it took her five years to pick herself up and put herself back together.

She glanced at the calendar on the wall. What would happen when Claire packed up her and Zoe's bags and headed to Tulsa at the end of summer?

Was there a Reece nugget of wisdom for that?

Outside, Reece parked his truck in the Ballard drive and sat for a moment.

"You okay, boss?"

"Yeah. Yeah, sure. I'm fine." Reece turned to

Willard, noting the genuine concern in the old cowboy's eyes.

"Didn't you have a family meeting this morning?"

"I did."

"Problems?" Willard asked.

"No. No problems." Reece shook his head, recalling the brief meeting. He and Tucker and Mitch sat at Reece's kitchen table with Kate on speakerphone. After a few false starts he'd shared that Zoe was his daughter.

As predicted, they were over the moon thrilled and ready to welcome her into the family fold. While Reece was relieved to get the secret out in the open, there wouldn't be any happy dances until he told Zoe that he was her absentee father.

Everything rested on whether his little girl forgave him.

"Something's got you worked up," Willard persisted. "Do you want to talk about it? I know I jest around mostly, but I'm a good ear if you need one."

Reece smiled, and while he found himself humbled by the offer, only the good Lord could help him now.

"I'm good," he finally said. "But I appreciate your concern."

Willard was a step and a half behind Reece as

they headed to the Ballard house, where he could see Claire wiping down the kitchen table.

His knock at the back door had her turning around with a jump.

"Sorry, didn't mean to startle you," he said through the screen. "I brought Willard. We have a small project to complete."

"A project? What project?"

"The swings I promised Zoe."

Willard trudged up the steps, removed his hat and offered a nod. "Afternoon, Ms. Ballard."

"Why, Willard, don't you look nice?"

Willard pointed to Reece. "He nabbed me before I could change out of church clothes."

"It's halfway to dinner, Cornell. Church let out hours ago. You were jawing with the ladies at the diner most of the afternoon."

"Ignore him," Willard said. "He's jealous because the ladies are partial to a mature gent."

Claire seemed to be biting back a chuckle. "Do you two want to come in for coffee?"

"I'd sure like to," Willard said.

Reece's hand shot out to block him. "We're not here for coffee."

"I don't know. Something sure smells good," Willard continued. "By the way, that peach bread was delicious, Ms. Ballard."

"I'm making cookies. I'll give you some to take home."

Willard nudged Reece with an elbow. "We need to come over here more often."

"You need to get those supplies out of the truck," Reece said.

"Yes, boss."

Claire inched closer to the door. "I thought we were going to…you know."

"We'll get to that. I've got Willard for two hours, so I figured I better keep my promise to Zoe to get those swings up ASAP."

"Swings!" Zoe soared into the room, arms wide like an airplane. "You said swings. I heard it."

"That's right," Reece said. He couldn't help but grin at the sight. Everything about Zoe lifted his heart.

"May I watch, Mommy?"

"Ask your…" She cleared her throat. "Ask Mr. Reece."

Ask your father? The near slip didn't escape him and he found himself grinning even wider.

"Mr. Reece, may I watch?" Zoe asked.

"If you follow our instructions, you may. We don't want any accidents in the construction site."

Zoe offered a solemn nod. "I promise."

The buzz of the saw and the sander had Claire constantly peeking out the door to see their progress and check on Zoe. She interrupted them half a dozen times before they finally finished the project.

When Reece stepped back to examine their handiwork, Zoe clapped her hands, pleased at the sight of the two swings hanging from the tree.

"Ready for a ride?" he asked.

She nodded eagerly and Reece helped her onto a seat. At the first push, delighted giggles rang out.

"Claire, come out here. We're done," he called.

She raced out the door and down the steps with Blue right behind her and a plastic container tucked under her arm.

"This is wonderful," Claire said. "May I?" She pointed to the other swing.

"Absolutely," Reece said.

She handed Willard the container before she sat on the smooth pine seat.

"What's this?" Willard asked.

"Christmas cookies."

"Ma'am, you know it's the middle of July, right?"

"I'm practicing for the party at the end of the month. This is my grandmother's sugar cookie recipe. They're delicious."

"In that case, I'll take them. I thought they were left over from last Christmas."

Claire laughed. "You're funny."

"Yeah, trouble is I don't mean to be."

For several moments Reece simply savored the sight of Claire and Zoe racing to swing higher than each other. Their carefree laughter filled the summer air and tugged at his heart.

"A fine sight, isn't it?" Willard leaned against another tree, grinning.

"It is," Reece agreed.

"I believe this is my cue to be on my way," the old cowboy said.

"Thanks," Reece said. "I appreciate all you've done around here. I mean that."

"Watching those two on that swing and knowing I don't have to share these cookies with anyone is all the thanks I need."

Reece chuckled as he pulled his keys from his pocket and tossed them to Willard. "I'll get a ride home from Claire."

It was a full thirty minutes before Claire and Zoe agreed to take a break from the swings and follow him into the house.

Reece washed his hands at the sink and eyed the coffeepot. "Mind if I help myself?" he asked Claire.

"I'll get it. It's the least I can do after all your hard work." She turned to Zoe. "Honey, go wash your hands and you can have a snack."

"How did it go with your family?" Claire asked once Zoe left the room.

"It was great. Just like I told you it would be."

"They aren't mad at me?"

"Mad? No. The hardest part was getting them to curb their enthusiasm. Mitch and Tucker were already brainstorming ways to welcome Zoe into the family."

"That's good, right?"

He laughed. "Yeah. Usually."

Claire slid the coffee in front of him. "I'm glad your family handled things so well, but I'm nervous," she whispered.

"Don't be. A week from now, today will just be a really good memory."

Claire stared at him for a moment. "That's a nice way to look at things. I can do that."

Reece took a long drink of coffee and wrapped his hands around the mug. "Okay, I'm nervous, too," he admitted.

When Claire reached down to put her hand on his arm, Reece froze.

"We've got this, Reece. It's going to be okay."

In that moment, he knew that it would be.

Zoe skipped back into the kitchen, her eyes on the plate of cookies on the counter.

"Sweetie, come and sit at the table with Mr. Reece and Mommy. Do you want some of these Christmas cookies I baked?"

"Yes, please."

Claire placed a glass of milk in front of Zoe and a plate of cookies in the middle of the table.

"Zoe, look at Mommy."

Zoe raised her head and wiped the milk from her lip with her tongue. "Am I in trouble?"

"No. Not at all."

"Then may I please have a cookie? I want that star with the red sprinkles."

"It's yours," Reece said. "But after we talk."

Zoe smiled up at him. "What do you want to talk about, Mr. Reece?"

"Zoe," Claire began. "Remember how you said that you want a daddy like Mr. Reece?"

"Uh-huh."

"Honey, Mr. Reece *is* your daddy."

Her mouth opened and her eyes fluttered in surprise. Slowly, Zoe turned to Reece. "You're really my daddy?"

Reece nodded and swallowed. He had never seen so much hope on one person's face.

"Where have you been?" Zoe asked. As she stared at him, her blue eyes welled with moisture. "I prayed to God every night for you to find me."

"I'm sorry, Zoe." He sucked in a breath of air, fighting for control. "But I'm here now."

"I've missed you so much." Zoe launched herself into his arms and buried her face in his neck.

Once the initial shock ended, Reece wrapped his arms around his daughter and patted her back.

Next to him, Claire swiped at the tears running down her face and looked away.

For a long minute, the room was silent. Then Zoe eased her arms from around his neck and stared at him with wonder.

Eyes rounded, she smiled. "Can I call you Daddy?"

Reece's heart stuttered. "Daddy would be really nice."

Zoe glanced from her plate of cookies to Reece. "Do you want some cookies, Daddy?"

"Yeah, let's have cookies, Zee."

With his free hand, Reece reached over and took Claire's hand in his. Her fingers were warm as they gently squeezed his. "Thank you, Claire," he murmured.

She wordlessly nodded and bit her lip.

The past and present had collided today. It was Zoe who paid the price for her parents' decisions. Now he could only pray they could move forward. There was no future in living in the past and he was more than ready to be a father to his daughter.

Chapter Eight

"Claire!"

Claire turned, her gaze scanning downtown Rebel.

Daisy waved from the other end of Main Street. In a flash, the redhead scooped a chubby toddler under her arm and racewalked a double stroller in Claire's direction. The woman had long legs.

"Where have you been?" Daisy put the golden-haired toddler down and handed her a box of raisins. All the while, Daisy's gaze never left Claire's.

"I… I haven't gone anywhere," Claire sputtered. She smiled at the shy, rosy-faced toddler and peeked in the stroller at the sleeping twins.

"I beg to differ," Daisy continued. "Mitch told me that Reece dropped the Zoe bombshell at a family meeting. Then you disappear from the face of the earth." She pushed loose spiral curls from her face and caught her breath. "Aren't we friends? Why didn't you tell me?"

Claire frowned and rubbed the bridge of her nose. "I wasn't sure anyone would be interested in being my friend once they found out that Reece didn't know he had a daughter and it was my fault." She took a slow breath. "Now I realize I was a coward, leaving Reece to tell his family by himself."

"First, let me say that this is a no-judgment zone. However, from what Mitch tells me, six years ago Reece was in no place to be anyone's daddy. I completely understand and respect you for putting Zoe first." She narrowed her eyes. "So you *have* been hiding from me."

"No. Not at all. Peach harvest is overlapping with the impending apple harvest. Then there's the Christmas-in-July event in a week. Plus, we're down a farm manager at the moment."

Claire glanced around. "This is for your ears only, but Asa Turner has been diagnosed with a tumor near his spine. The biopsy is this week." She paused. Just saying the words out loud was difficult. "Please keep him in your prayers."

"Yes. I'll have my prayer group get right on this. No names, but we can still storm the heavens on his behalf."

"Thank you."

"Where's Zoe today?" Daisy asked.

"Reece has her while I run errands. And I've been running errands all day."

"I guess you have been busy." Daisy clucked her tongue. "However, that does not excuse you from a welcome-to-the-family hug."

"I'm not family. Zoe is."

"Details. Come here." Daisy wrapped her arms around Claire.

Claire couldn't remember the last time she was hugged. Daisy smelled like vanilla bean and baby powder. It was nice to have someone like Daisy in her life.

"I've never met anyone like you," Claire said. "You're such an unconditional friend."

"Isn't that the way it's supposed to be? I don't need fair-weather friends. Do you?"

"No. You're right. An anomaly, but definitely right." Claire smiled at the other woman.

"We're sisters of the heart," Daisy said. "I knew that when I first met you, Claire. But, if you don't mind me saying so, I think you're going about things all wrong with Reece."

"I'm sorry—" Claire blinked "—what?"

"Reece likes you and I haven't seen you make any effort whatsoever to reel the man in."

"I don't know what to say to that. Reece and I are friends." She nodded, mentally affirming her words. Yes, almost two months working together on the farm had established a comfortable rapport. That was good enough for her. Wasn't it?

"Friends? Claire, seriously, let's review the facts. Reece hasn't let the family meet anyone he's dating. Ever."

"We're not dating."

"Let me finish." Daisy held up a palm. "From the moment you hit town, he's chosen to spend time with you. Starting your first weekend here, when he helped you at the Rebel Farmers Market."

"This is all about his daughter, Daisy."

"I know plenty of couples with children who share custody. They do not hang around with each other on purpose."

"Reece and I have gotten reacquainted after a bumpy past, but we spend time together because of Zoe and my father's will."

"Yes. That's another thing." Daisy's expression registered confusion. "Why didn't Reece just buy the farm from you?"

"Probably because he knew I'd take off for Tulsa the minute the ink was dry, and he wanted us to get to know each other again. For Zoe." Claire shrugged. "It worked. We've become solid friends. I have great respect for Reece and that's all there is to it."

"Pastor's wife at your three o'clock."

"What are you talking about?"

"Add the egg whites and beat until they're glossy and hold a firm peak," Daisy said with a nod. "That's the secret."

Claire blinked and looked around. "Oh, hello, Mrs. Tuttle."

"Honey, you call me Saylor. Everyone does." Saylor Tuttle patted her Dolly Parton hairdo. "Daisy, I don't know what you're making, but I want some."

"Meringue, ma'am. It's all about the egg whites."

"Carry on, ladies."

Claire watched the pastor's wife move down the street before she turned to Daisy. "You're good," she said.

"The first commandment for life in Rebel. Thou shall not feed the grapevine." Daisy chuckled. "As I was saying, I know how it is when there are a lot of obstacles to a relationship, believe me. But it's worth it in the end."

"What is?"

"True love."

"True love?" Claire gasped. No. No. No. Reece hadn't given any indication he thought of her as anything but Zoe's mother.

"Reece is sweet, kind, generous to a fault and handsome," Daisy said. Pure admiration laced her words.

She had a point there. Reece was all those things and more.

"What's not to swoon over?" Daisy continued with a mischievous glint in her eyes.

"Daisy! You're married."

"I'm not blind. The Rainbolts come from good stock. Every one of them is God-fearing, easy on the eyes and a plain nice person. Mitch is the handsomest, but Reece comes in a close second."

Claire couldn't help but laugh, though clearly Reece was the most handsome Rainbolt brother.

"Mommy, I'm done."

Daisy took the raisin box and handed the golden-haired little girl a wet wipe without even blinking. Then she peeked in at the sleeping babies and checked her cell phone for messages.

"What was I saying?"

"This is PJ, right?" Claire was only too eager to distract Daisy from the topic at hand.

"Right! Little Patti Jo. She's named after my great-aunt. They're equal amounts of sweet and ornery." Daisy patted PJ's head. "Mitch calls this one obedience-challenged."

Once again Claire laughed. "I like Mitch's way with words."

Daisy grinned. "Me, too."

"And the babies are Dawn and Dana," Claire said. "They're always smiling. Even in their sleep."

"My dear husband says that's more to do with digestion issues than anything. He's wrong, of course." Daisy laughed. "But I have to say, you're good. Most people ask for a scorecard when it comes to my children. In truth, most days I run through everyone's names before I remember the name of the child I am speaking to."

"I'm a nurse. I have to remember a dozen patients' names and histories every shift. I lean on mnemonics."

"Brilliant. You'll need that trick now that you're in the family. It's hard to believe that the Rainbolts started out with five kids in a trailer and now they're multiplying like rabbits. With you and Zoe, we're up to sixteen."

Claire opened her mouth and closed it. It seemed best not to remind Daisy, once again, that she wasn't family. "Where are the rest of your children?"

"Summer day camp at the Rebel Community Center. It's only a half day and you get to pick your courses. Grace is taking dance. Seth astronomy. Christian and Sam are in a group class that's taking a field trip to Tulsa today."

"Really?"

"Uh-huh. Maybe Zoe might like to check it out." Daisy dug in her diaper bag and pulled out a bag of lemons. "Could you hold this?"

Claire's gaze met hers as she grabbed the fruit.

"Don't ask," Daisy said. She rummaged for a moment before finding a brochure. "Here's the schedule. I have another one of these at home. Keep it."

"Painting?" Claire handed back the lemons and flipped the pages of the brochure. "And it's not too late to sign up?"

"No. Not at all. It's totally drop-in. Grace took painting last summer. She loved it."

"I'll have to talk to Zoe about this. Thank you, Daisy."

"You're welcome. Oh, and I nearly forgot. I got your invitation to the party. Now tell me what I can bring."

"May I be so bold as to ask for Daisy's pies? Yours are the best."

"Why thank you." She smiled. "So you want the three Ps?"

"What's the three Ps?"

"Pumpkin, pecan and peach!"

Claire burst out laughing. "Yes. Please. That sounds wonderful."

"How many guests?"

"You won't believe it, but the numbers have swelled to twenty-four."

Daisy waved a hand. "I've got you covered, my friend."

"Luna Diaz, the chef from Rebel Ranch, is bringing Bûche de Noël, although I haven't had a minute to figure out what that is."

"Yule log," Daisy said. "Think yummy. Hers are a work of art."

"Yummy is my favorite recipe."

"What else do you have planned?" Daisy asked.

"Reece is doing most of the planning."

"Reece, the guy who is only your friend? That Reece?"

Claire stared at Daisy for a moment. Was it so unusual for Reece to be helping with the planning?

"Go ahead. I didn't mean to interrupt."

"This is my very first dinner party. I'm overwhelmed."

Daisy waved a hand in dismissal. "Don't be. Everyone will pitch in. You'll see." She grinned wide and grabbed Claire's hand. "This is such a great idea. I can't believe I didn't think of it myself."

"Next year it's yours."

"Does that mean you'll be here next year?"

Claire froze at the question. "I honestly don't know."

Daisy patted her arm. "Relax. You don't have to decide now. Of course, I want you to stay but if you don't, I know where to find you."

"Thanks, Daisy."

"Now where are you off to?"

"I'm meeting Reece and Zoe at Rebel Ranch."

Daisy's lips twitched.

"Don't say it. He's just showing me the ranch.

I've managed to avoid it until now, because I'm not a fan of horses."

"Oh, it's not so bad. It's also not so good. I am not a horse person, either. Give me a cat any day."

"Say a prayer, would you?"

"I will, and remember that the ranch has a perfectly good UTV. Reece can show you around in that. You don't ever have to ride a horse. I never have."

"Thank you for that bit of information."

"My pleasure. We gals have to stick together."

Claire found herself smiling as she walked to her car. Across the street, someone waved at her. It was Zoe's Sunday school teacher. Claire waved back.

She was going to miss this little town if she left. *When* she left, she corrected herself. And then out of nowhere her conversation with Reece taunted her.

I'm torn between two worlds. My father's and mine.

Maybe you need to consider Zoe's world.

Was he right?

"She's here, boss."

Reece turned at Willard's voice. His gaze followed the little hybrid as it rounded the bend in the ranch road. His pulse quickened like a young kid when she put her hand out the window and waved.

He'd been looking forward to Claire visiting the ranch for weeks. She'd bailed on him the last time they'd scheduled because of the peach harvest. It was true, the farm was busier than even he could have predicted. Still, he had the niggling feeling she didn't want to come to Rebel Ranch and he couldn't figure out why.

Claire drove her little hybrid in, got out and glanced around. She wore jeans and a pretty pink T-shirt and her dark hair was loose around her shoulders, the way he liked it. Not that she knew his preference, he admonished himself. Or cared.

Still, she had a smile on her face and he'd take that as a good sign.

"Ms. Ballard. Good to see you," Willard said.

"Willard, I'm testing sweet potato casserole for the party. Think you can stop by this week and try some?"

"It'll be a chore, but I'm willing to do that for you since we've gotten to be such good friends."

Claire laughed and the sound reminded Reece of Zoe.

"Hi, Reece," she said.

"Claire. Glad you could make it."

"Anything you need me for, boss?" Willard asked. "If not, I've got plans in town."

"Rebel, Oklahoma, on a payday Friday. Have fun."

"Yes, sir." He tipped his hat in Claire's direction before heading to his truck.

"So, Reece," Claire said. "I wanted to talk to you about my friends."

"I already took care of it. They arrive Friday night, before the party, and leave Sunday morning. Friend-and-family discount." He met her gaze. "Claire, you've told me six times. Now go ahead and cross it off your list and trust me that it's done."

"Thank you."

"I also threw in a free massage and they'll have access to a private riding lesson if they choose."

"A massage and a trail ride. That's so nice of you."

He looked at her. "I can comp the entire stay if you like."

Her eyes rounded in confusion. "Why would you do that?"

"They're your friends."

"But they aren't your friends."

"Claire, Zoe is family and you're her mother."

"How do you make any money with that logic?"

Reece stared at her and then belly laughed. "We're doing just fine, thanks."

"I think the discount is plenty, but I appreciate the offer."

"No problem. Now how about I show you the ranch?"

Claire glanced around. "Where's Zoe?"

"She wants to be a chef when she grows up, so I have her spending the next hour with Luna Diaz in our ranch kitchen. They're going to make cookies or something."

"She's with the ranch chef?"

"That's right."

Claire's eyes lit up and a soft smile touched her lips. The effect made Reece remember how much he liked to make her smile.

"That's so nice of you. I'm sure she'd delighted."

"Yeah, she was doing that little shoulder scrunch thing she does when she's happy."

"Don't you love when she does that? It's so adorable."

"Yeah, it is," he said. "Almost as good as when she tries to wheedle something out of me with that pretty-please look. That girl's going to be a handful when she's older."

"I say that about ten times a day."

Claire smiled and then paused as if suddenly realizing that they were swapping kid tales, like two normal parents. She cleared her throat. "So it's just us?"

"Is that okay? I want to show you the ranch, Claire."

"I don't have to ride a horse?"

At her words, the penny slid through the slot and he nearly palm-smacked his forehead. Why hadn't he figured it out earlier? Claire was opposed to any situation where she wasn't in control of the outcome. To someone who'd never ridden, horses had a great big danger sign on them.

"Nope. We can use the UTV."

Her shoulders relaxed. "That would be wonderful."

"This way." Claire followed him to the other side of the barn where two bright green utility vehicles sans doors were parked.

"I tried to talk my father into one of these the first time I saw someone from the ranch driving over the pasture with it. I was vetoed."

"Why, do you suppose?" He pointed to the first vehicle and got in.

"Maybe the cost or maybe he didn't like change. Probably a little of both." Claire slid into the passenger seat and fastened the seat belt.

"And he didn't ride?"

"No. Not interested in horses at all. We used the old ranch jeep or the tractor to get around."

"People can get stuck in their ways. I get that," Reece said. He backed up the vehicle and headed out.

"Where are we going?"

"There's a place I want to show you, way out in the north forty."

"That sign we just passed." She pointed. "Pond Road. What's that?"

Reece backed up the UTV and headed down the road she mentioned. "Look there, through the weeping willow."

Claire gasped. "That's not a pond. It's a lake. It even has a pier. How did you make that happen?"

"Good planning?"

"No, seriously. I can't believe there's a lake—here on Rebel Ranch."

"I am serious. It's man-made. Sure we have a couple natural ponds on the ranch, like the one Blue favors. But this is different."

"If it's a lake, why do you call it Pond Road?"

"Because city folk like the notion of a pond."

Claire frowned. "What do you use it for?"

He laughed. "What do you think we use if for? It's for fishing. We stock it for guests. Then we had to put up the signs because they seemed to get lost on their own."

"Wait a minute. Are you telling me you have a lake on the ranch stocked with fish?"

"Yep. It's one of the many attractions offered to our guests. I should have given you the color brochure. Haven't you looked at our website? Tucker and Violet did that. It has more bells and whistles than I can count."

"Are you kidding? The internet is so slow at the farm that I time-out when I check my email."

"That's not good. Remind me and we'll take care of that, too."

"Okay, but I'd rather go fishing than check my email."

Reece stopped the vehicle. "You fish?" He couldn't believe his ears. Claire Ballard, the princess who lived in the big old Ballard house, went fishing?

"I was raised on a farm. Yes, I fish. Come on, what better bonding time for a farmer who doesn't like to talk than to take his daughter to a fishing hole and tell her to be quiet or she'll scare the fish away."

She offered a sad shake of her head. "I cannot tell you the number of times I fell for that. Along the way, I learned how to fish and read a book at the same time."

Reece looked at her and his chest ached. He may have had some kind of pathetic childhood but he had Mitch, Tucker, Kate and Levi. They had each other. Claire didn't have anyone.

He couldn't help himself. Reece reached out and squeezed Claire's hand. "I'm glad you fish. You and I will go fishing sometime. And, Claire, I promise you can talk all you want."

"I'd like that." She smiled. "You know, Reece, my father was a good man and these past weeks have given me clarity on a few things. I'm now able to see the farm with the eyes of an adult and a businesswoman and not as that angry daughter."

"What's that mean, Claire?"

"I've just come to the point where I realize my father was a man. That he was doing his best for me and for the farm and maybe that's what I need to focus on."

They drove another mile or so, past the cattle in the back pasture. Claire straightened in her seat and stared at the beasts grazing in the July heat. "How many did you say you have?"

"A dozen, give or take, depending on the time of year. We move them back and forth and let the guests pretend they're on a trail ride. They love it and it helps us rotate the pasture."

"You bring in your own hay?"

"That's in the works. Right now, we buy local and pray the prices don't go up."

He steered the UTV over a hill to the edge of a thick circle of conifers.

"What's here?"

"Come on. I'll show you." He got out of the vehicle and she followed.

The ground cover beneath the trees crackled with the sound of dried pine needles.

"I hear water," Claire said.

Indeed, the sound of water trickling over stones could be heard through the trees. When they stepped out of the dark cover of the pine branches into the clearing, the creek greeted them with its rhythmic gurgles.

"You have a creek." Her voice reflected awe.

This was his creek. Always had been. No one else had the patience to wander this far on the land just for a little stream of water. This was where Reece came to think, to mourn and to pray. This was where he heard God as he lay on his back in the warm grass, staring up at the clouds that floated past.

"Rebel Ranch is like a paradise, isn't it? You have a little bit of everything."

Yeah, it was a paradise. He'd always thought the same thing. Her words wrapped around him. "You think so?"

"I do."

"I don't allow the guests out this far. It's sort of sacred ground to me."

She looked at the water and then up at him. "Mind if I sit on the rocks and put my feet in the water?"

"I do it all the time. Go ahead."

Claire slipped off her sneakers and tiptoed to the bank.

"Watch your step. The stones can be slick."

"I'll be careful."

Water flowed around her ankles and she leaned

back on her elbows, eyes closed with her face to the sun. "I could sit here forever."

"Thought that a time or two myself." Mesmerized, he could hardly draw himself away from the sight of Claire sitting at his creek. Never once had his too-big dreams included this.

Reece reached down and plucked a flat blade of long grass. Cupping his hands together, he lined up the grass with his thumbs and blew air through the blade. A high pitch whistle cut through the silence.

Claire turned toward the sound and smiled. "That was really good. You have to show Zoe how to do that."

Yeah, Zoe would love to grass whistle. He blew once more.

"Tell me about this place," Claire said as she threaded water through her fingers.

"It was here before there was anything else on Rebel Ranch. When the guest ranch was something in my head that I hadn't even figured out how to make a reality."

"Why did you bring me out here?"

"Because I need you to understand something."

Claire pulled her feet from the water and walked to stand in front of him. "Tell me."

He took a long uneven breath as he struggled to gather his courage. "I, um… I lost hope when my brother died. I came out here and I flat gave up. My dream was this ranch—turning it into something we could pass on to our children, like Gramps passed it on to us." He rubbed his chin and swallowed. "Everything fell apart when Levi died." He tossed the blade of grass to the ground and crushed it beneath his boot.

Silence hung between them, but Claire waited patiently for him to continue and he waited for the wave of emotion to subside.

"I know I was in a bad way when we ran into each other in Tulsa. But I need you to know that what I felt for you then was real. You're the most amazing woman I've ever known."

Claire's eye widened a bit and she took a sharp breath of air.

"I ran off because I was afraid. Scared to death that you would find out I was just a dreamer. Mostly, I was terrified it was the truth. The poor kid from the wrong side of town pretending he could make something of himself." He clenched his fists at his side and looked away.

"Oh, Reece." She touched his arm.

"You just need to know that it was never about you. You're golden, Claire. It was all about me."

"Stop. Stop putting me on a pedestal. I have flaws you don't even know about." She gave an annoyed shake of her head. "Why do you do that?"

"Do what?"

"Act like you're a going nowhere cowboy."

"Claire, I am almost forty years old and no matter what I accomplish I'll never be an educated man."

"Not going to college is what torments you? From where I'm sitting, looking down at Rebel Ranch, you've built an empire." She shrugged. "Besides, you can do whatever you want to do. If somehow in your mind you believe a college education is what you need, then go for it. You are never too old to go after what you imagine is holding you back."

He scoffed. "I'm way too old for college."

"You are not." She lifted her chin.

"What are you thinking?" he asked.

A long silence separated them until Claire met his gaze. "I'm trying to figure out why you really decided to tell me all this today."

"Because I don't want the way I treated you in the past to be the reason that you leave now."

"I see. So this is all about me leaving and taking Zoe?" Her gaze hardened. "You weren't talking about us."

"Claire, I wouldn't begin to presume that after all this time and my poor behavior you would have feelings for me. It's enough that you've forgiven me."

"What about you, Reece? What do you feel after all this time?"

"I care about you, Claire. I can't deny that. I always have. Maybe I always will."

"Thank you for bringing me here and for telling me," she said. "It makes it hurt a little less in some ways and makes it hurt much more when I think of all the years of misunderstanding that stood between us because of our misperceptions."

"Where do we go from here?" he asked.

"All I know is that I am willing to agree that maybe there are options that I hadn't considered. Or hadn't been willing to consider."

Reece listened to her words intently. For the first time in a long time, he took a deep breath and dared to hope. Yeah, he would hope and then he'd file away the memory of today, just in case he needed it someday.

Chapter Nine

"My list. Where is my list?" Claire did a complete circle in the living room, searching beneath the holiday garlands that lined the mantel and then around the electric candles on the window-sills.

"Here it is, Mommy. Blue had it." Zoe held up a shredded paper with evidence of slobber.

"Ew." Claire carefully plucked the scrap of paper from her daughter and dumped it in the trash can. "Please wash your hands."

She pointed at Blue. "You're going into the guest bedroom for the night, mister."

Minutes later, Zoe returned. She danced across the living room and then curtsied, the tulle under-skirt of her dress billowing as she moved. "I love Christmas dresses."

"You look so pretty."

"Red and green. Christmas colors."

"That's right."

"Ho. Ho. Ho. Anyone home?"

Claire turned at the sound of Reece's voice. "Come in. The door is open."

"Hey, those lights outside look really great. Who strung them for you?"

"Willard. It's amazing how much mileage I get out of homemade peppermint bark."

He ducked beneath the mistletoe that hung between the kitchen and living room, his gaze searching hers. "Wow, you look absolutely beautiful."

"Which one of us?" Claire asked.

"Both of you."

Zoe giggled and rushed Reece. "Thank you, Daddy."

"You look pretty nice, too, Reece."

He wore new jeans and a dress coat with a shirt and tie. The scruff on his face was gone and his hair without a hat had been neatly combed. Claire touched his ridiculously gaudy holiday tie and shook her head.

"This is an interesting tie," she said. "I would have expected it from Willard, but you?"

"Hey, it's a conversation starter." Laughter sparkled in his eyes and a teasing grin touched his mouth.

She couldn't help but smile in return. It was

nice to be able to tease and be teased without the usual tension between them.

Reece glanced around the living room. "Look at this place."

Claire's gaze followed his and scrutinized the room.

"Where did you find poinsettia and mistletoe in July?"

"It's not as difficult as you might think. You can buy anything on the internet. I could have rented dancing reindeer if I'd had the urge."

"Thank you for exercising restraint."

"Tell me what you really think, Reece? Is it too much? What about the music?"

He inclined an ear. "Not loud enough."

"I can fix that."

"Other than that, it's great." His gaze met hers and he stared intently. "What's not to love?"

Claire let her breath go in a rush as her heart did a little dance.

"Do you like the angel on top of the tree?" Zoe asked.

"I do. It's beautiful. Hey, I nearly forgot. I brought you something."

"Really?" Zoe lit up at her father's words.

"Merry Christmas in July, Zee." He handed her a small gold package with a little red bow.

Her blue eyes rounded and she released a soft

breath of surprise. "A present! Mommy, you said no presents because it's only pretend Christmas."

"Oops." Reece shrugged with mock chagrin.

"You're quite the rule-breaker," Claire murmured. Yet, how could she deny him? The man had missed so many Christmases with his daughter.

"May I open it now?" Zoe's gaze went from her mother to her father.

"Your call, Reece," Claire said.

"I say…" He paused and grinned. "Open it."

She tore into the package until a small velvet box appeared. "What is it?"

Claire took the box from Zoe's fingers and opened the hinges before handing it back to her. Nestled on a bed of navy velvet was a silver chain with a small charm engraved with the letter *z*.

"Oh, it's beautiful," Zoe breathed. "May I wear it?"

Reece nodded and took the necklace from the box. Claire held Zoe's hair back as he fastened it around her neck.

"This is like a big girl necklace." She opened her arms for a hug and Reece swept her into his arms and twirled her around.

"Because you are a big girl."

When he put her back on the ground, she laughed. "I'm going up to my room to see in the mirror."

"That was a very thoughtful gift," Claire said.

"Thank you." He nodded toward her outfit. "Nice dress."

She glanced down at the simple red sheath. "Do you think so?"

"Claire, surely you realize how beautiful you are. I'm guessing that lots of guys have told you."

His eyes met hers and once again she warmed beneath his scrutiny. "Reece, I haven't dated lots of guys."

He frowned. "I guess we never talked about it, but I assumed… Six years is a long time without a date."

"It's a personal decision. There is no right or wrong. Frankly, I'm much too tired to date. I work the night shift."

"Not a single date?"

"Coffee or meeting with a group of friends." She looked at him. "What about you?" she asked, pretending his answer didn't matter.

"I've been creating something from nothing with my family's inheritance. Doesn't leave much time for anything else."

"Daisy said you didn't bring your dates home to meet the family."

"Oh, that Daisy. She's something else. I didn't bring anyone home because there wasn't anyone to meet."

His gaze was pointed, and she knew what he

was thinking, because she'd thought about him a time or two at the end of a long day of working side by side in the orchard. Then she dismissed the notion.

"I haven't allowed myself to go there, Reece. Right now, it's all about one day at a time."

"You said the same thing on your birthday."

"Did I?"

"Yeah, and that was weeks ago. You know it can't hurt to see if we have a foundation for something more this time."

He was wrong. It could hurt. It could hurt more than it did the last time, because this time she had more invested than she did years ago.

No, she wasn't going there. Especially not tonight when she could so easily be lured by how breathtakingly handsome he looked with that Rainbolt charm all over him.

"I'm going to go grab the hors d'oeuvres from the stove," Claire said.

"Hors d'oeuvres, huh? What's on the menu?"

"Daisy says no Christmas party is complete without tiny hotdogs wrapped in bacon and stuffed mushrooms."

"I guess Daisy would know." He smiled. "What can I do to help?"

"I'd be grateful if you'd lure Blue into the room next to Zoe's with his water dish and close the door."

"That I can handle." He paused. "Hey, I heard your friend made it in."

"Yes. Only one of them. There's a big certification inspection Monday at the hospital, so the powers that be decided not to allow them both off at the same time. One of them had to stay and audit charts over the weekend."

"That's too bad."

"I'm grateful Tracey made it. We've known each other a long time, and she's a single mom, too."

"Does she know?"

"That you're Zoe's father? Yes, I told her and she's thrilled for you and Zoe."

"What about you? Is she thrilled for you? No more single parenting. You can share the load now."

"I'm still wrapping my head around that one."

The front doorbell rang and Claire jumped. She clasped her hands together. "Oh, my. It's starting."

"Claire, you got this." Reece winked at her. "I'll get Blue."

Two hours later, Claire cornered Reece in the kitchen as he started to make another pot of coffee. "How many people did you invite?"

"You sent out the invitations." He continued to carefully measure grounds into the filter.

"I didn't send one to the librarian."

After hitting Start, he turned around. "Which librarian?"

"The tall gentleman telling avian jokes."

"Avian jokes?"

"What do you give a sick bird?" Claire paused. "A tweet-ment."

"Oh, boy." Reece walked to the doorway and looked around the living room. "Where?"

Claire moved next to him and cocked her head to the right. "Over there, by the tree. The one swaying to 'Jingle Bell Rock' and talking to my friend Tracey."

"Oh, that's Nate. I don't know who invited him. You can tell Tracey that he's single."

"I just said that he tells bird jokes."

"Nobody's perfect. Besides, it's Christmas in July. Where's your goodwill toward man?"

"Hey, you two," Daisy called.

Both Claire and Reece turned to see the redhead grinning and pointing at the ceiling. Claire glanced up.

Mistletoe.

She looked at Reece and cringed.

"It's no big deal," he said. "If you act like it's a big deal, everyone is going to stop talking and look at us."

He was right. Not a big deal. She inched up on her toes and kissed his lips. Then her eyes flew open. Reece was kissing her back. Claire stepped back in stunned surprise and didn't dare glance over to see who was looking. She turned around and reached for the closest candy dish. "Peppermint bark, anyone?"

"That was a very good kiss." Tracey hooked her arm through Claire's and tugged her aside. "If you're taking orders, I'll take peppermint bark and one of him."

Claire inspected the candy dish, praying her warm face had cooled. "Reece? Didn't I introduce you?"

"You did not. Although I caught a long glimpse of him when I checked in at the ranch. I thought I was going to have to give myself CPR when I turned and saw a cowboy on a black horse with a black Stetson. The receptionist said he owns Rebel Ranch."

"His family does."

"Now I find out that the man is not only Zoe's father but he is taken."

"I don't believe he is."

Tracey gave her a playful elbow nudge. "Please," she drawled.

"What are you getting at?" Her gaze met her friend's.

"You know what I'm talking about. Come on, you have it all here in Rebel. This farm is a fabulous opportunity for you and Zoe. There's a cowboy hunk next door who happens to be your daughter's daddy, and said cowboy hunk fancies you. Why would you go back to Tulsa?"

"My job."

"Nursing jobs are a dime a dozen or less. Besides, I heard that our dear supervisor is already interviewing for your position. By the way, she's been a nightmare since you left."

"Interviewing?" Claire groaned. "She can't do that."

"Actually, she can. It's legal. You're on a personal leave of absence not a medical leave. You'll be slotted into another position when and if you return because you're that good."

"I can't believe this," Claire returned.

Tracey nodded in sympathy. "I checked with HR on your behalf when I found out yesterday. Just some general questions. Your position has been posted and the application period closes in thirty days." She frowned. "It stinks, but there's nothing you can do except get back to town and reapply for your position, or embrace the opportunity that God has dropped on your doorstep here in Rebel." She leaned close. "If the poll is open, I vote for here."

"Tracey, I worked hard for that job. She could have at least notified me of her decision. That's common courtesy."

"Tell me about it. But are you going to live on five hours of sleep a night indefinitely? Keep the farm, Claire. I'm telling you, I'll visit and we can have playdates. I would never give up the chance for happiness with the cowboy and your daughter for a stethoscope in Tulsa."

"Claire? Asa and Nan are looking for you before they leave."

Claire turned at Daisy's voice.

"Oh, sure. Be right there."

Tracey tugged on her arm. "Think about it."

"I will."

An hour later as guests trickled out the door, thanking Claire for a fun party, she was still thinking about Tracey's words. Waving goodbye to the disappearing lights of the last car, she slipped off her heels and searched for her daughter.

"Zoe?" Claire wandered back to the living room.

"Shh. She's here."

Reece sat on the couch with Zoe curled up next to him asleep. His gaze moved from the Christmas tree to Claire. "Do you remember any of those ornaments from when you were a kid?"

She eased down onto the couch. "Not a one."

"Beautiful tree."

"Yes." She glanced at the artificial tree decorated with vintage ornaments and twinkling white lights, topped with a golden angel. "I didn't even use all the ornaments in the attic. There were too many."

"Save them for when Zoe grows up." He stroked his daughter's hair from her face and smiled. "She had a good time."

Claire nodded absently as she silently memorized the scene before her. If she left, there wouldn't be any more nights like this.

"What about you?" she finally asked. "Did you have a good time?"

Claire took a tiny peek at the profile of the man who had left her breathless under the mistletoe.

"Best Christmas-in-July party of my entire life," he said.

"Your first one, too?"

"Yeah. But I got so many compliments on my tie that I think I could be persuaded to come again next year." He turned to her. "Daisy said she's hosting. Put it on your calendar."

"I'll do that."

"What about you, Claire? Did you have a good time?"

"Once I realized that no one really cared if there were dirty punch glasses in the sink, I had a great time."

His eyes shone with amusement as he smiled. "I'm glad."

"Nan told me that the sale in the market today was a huge success. The two-for-one deal sold out and everyone raved about the Ballard Farm logo swag we gave away."

"Even better. Now five hundred people are walking around with advertising for Ballard Farm produce."

"We're closing the market tomorrow," Claire said. "In fact, from now on, the market will be closed on Sunday. Ballard Farm should have a day of rest. To honor the Lord in all we do."

"Your idea?" he asked.

Claire nodded.

"I think that's an excellent idea. See, you're a very astute businesswoman. Work hard with sufficient staff when you're open and know when to rest. That's the best advice there is."

"I learned from you."

"What's next on our agenda?" he asked.

Our. She liked the sound of that.

"Asa's biopsy results will be in soon, maybe tomorrow, and I'll be interviewing possible assistant orchard production managers."

"Have you reviewed those résumés I dropped off?" he asked.

"I did." She looked at him. "You're going to help me with the final selection, right?"

"If you want me to."

"I do. Oh, and don't forget that the dedication at the community center is next Saturday."

"Good thing you only reminded me four times. I'll be there."

"Will you?"

He met her gaze. "Yeah, Claire, I will. I always keep my word."

On the second floor, Blue's whines could be heard.

"I'd better take Blue out," she said.

"I'll get Zoe up to bed." He stood, then leaned over and gently pressed a kiss to her forehead. "Merry Christmas in July, Claire."

"Merry Christmas," she murmured, while tucking away the promise his kiss offered.

The room seemed chilly once Reece and Zoe left, and Claire shivered, wrapping her arms around herself. A niggle of dread loomed, and she had to chase it away. *Stop worrying*, she told herself. *Everything is going to be fine.*

Claire hummed Christmas carols as she pulled decorations off the mailbox and retrieved the day's mail. What a gorgeous day. Even the Oklahoma humidity couldn't get her down. There were too many things to be grateful for.

Air-conditioning. Leftover Christmas cookies. A successful peach harvest.

When the Ballard Farm truck pulled into the drive, she offered a wave to Nan.

"Hi, Claire. Excellent party." Nan got out of the

truck and smiled. "I was just in town and everyone is talking about it."

"Yes, somehow everyone in town was represented, including a handful of party crashers, as well."

"That's just too funny. I suppose you should be honored. People only crash fun parties."

"I guess." She chuckled.

"I tried to call you," Nan continued. "But it went to voice mail."

"Oh, I've been taking down decorations. What's up?" Then Claire remembered. The biopsy results. She sucked in a breath, bracing for the news. "Is Asa okay?"

"More than okay. I just dropped him off at home."

"The biopsy results?"

"Benign." The word was uttered with a sigh of relief.

"Oh, thank You, Lord."

"Amen." Nan wiped away a tear before she reached out to embrace Claire. "Thank you for your prayers."

"That was the least I could do after all you and Asa have done for me. What did the doctor say?"

"It's a fatty tumor pressing on the nerves near his spine that's causing the pain. So surgery will still happen, but the doctor anticipates a full recovery."

"Wonderful news."

"Even better, because thanks to you and Reece, our workload has lightened significantly. It will be nice to have manageable hours again."

"You know it's mostly Reece, right? He's brought on the extra staff and has come up with the creative management ideas."

"Don't you dare sell yourself short, Claire Ballard. You've been working as hard as he has and you've had some terrific ideas."

"Maybe now you and Asa can think about the *V* word?"

Nan cocked her head "What's that?"

"Vacation."

The older woman's expression was doubtful. "Do farmers take vacations? I suppose it could happen." Nan looked toward the house. "Is Zoe inside?"

"She and Reece went to Pawhuska this morning for a book signing. His favorite cookbook author. He was determined to get Zoe an autographed cookbook."

"Those two are inseparable, aren't they?"

"Zoe does love spending time with Reece." But inseparable? Claire hadn't thought of it that way. Maybe it was truer than she realized. Or wanted to realize.

"She's still talking about being a chef, huh?"

"All the time."

"Dreams are a good thing."

"Yes. They are."

Dream big, Reece said. Claire smiled at the words.

"I expect I'll see you before Saturday," Nan said as she headed up the drive to the market building. "But I just want you to know that Asa and I are real excited about this honor for your father."

"Me, too. It seems sort of surreal that after the ceremony every time I drive past the community center I'll see his name up there. He was a good man, and he loved this town. I know he'd be both embarrassed and proud if he were here today."

Claire tucked the mail under her arm and grabbed a huge red-velvet Christmas bow from the mailbox.

Dumping everything in her arms on the kitchen table, her attention was drawn to the Christmas tree in the living room. What was the protocol for taking down Christmas-in-July trees? She wanted to keep it up a little longer and imagine what it was like when she was a child celebrating Christmas in this very room with her mother and father. Reaching a hand to the branches, she cradled a glass star in one hand and examined the sheen of the ornament. For a moment, she closed her eyes and reminded herself that there were good memories still to be nudged out of this house. Would it be such a bad idea to stick around to see them?

She grabbed a step stool and took down the mistletoe ball on her way back into the kitchen, adding it to the collection of decorations she'd piled on the table.

It was time for a break and time to answer the lure of leftover Christmas cookies on the counter. She filled a dessert plate with an assortment and poured coffee into a mug. There were still far too many left. The rest would go to Willard.

When she slid into the chair, the mistletoe ball taunted her, daring her to remember the kiss from last night. Claire touched her lips. As far as kisses, it had been a very good one and definitely kept her awake last night replaying the scene.

With a shake of her head, she gave herself a mental chastising. Mustn't read too much into one kiss—especially one that had happened under mistletoe.

Instead, Claire bit into a soft sugar cookie and retrieved the mail from beneath a shimmery gold garland. Examining each piece, she tore open an envelope from an attorney in Tulsa and unfolded the crisp letter inside. No doubt more Ballard Farm business.

Except it wasn't.

It was a draft custody agreement. The paper fluttered to the table when Claire slumped back in the chair, both of her hands over her mouth. She couldn't breathe. Couldn't think.

Please review the tentative terms and call the office at your convenience to arrange a time to meet with our client, Mr. Reece Rainbolt.

Why hadn't he told her he was moving forward with custody? Weren't they supposed to wait until the end of summer? Talk about the next steps. Plan what was best for Zoe.

There went her trust in Reece's promises.

A thousand thoughts raced through her mind at once and she grabbed a piece of paper and a pen and started a list.

First and foremost, she had to reapply for her supervisory position before the application-processing period closed. If not, then thirty days from now she'd be dealing with a pay cut and sitting in an empty apartment in Tulsa, wondering what to do with her life while her daughter was with her father, the primary custodian.

Oh, she'd already looked up the law in Oklahoma. What was in the best interest of the minor child? That was the question she asked herself over and over again.

Why wouldn't the courts agree to Reece taking over? He had money and power and could offer Zoe acres of green grass, fifteen Rainbolts as family and assorted animals around to love her.

Claire had a night-shift position and a small apartment. Not even a cat.

She groaned aloud. "This cannot be happening."

When a car door slammed shut, Claire stood, her knees shaking. Reece and Zoe were back.

"Look what I got!" Zoe raced into the kitchen with a brightly colored cookbook clutched to her chest.

"Oh, Zoe, that's wonderful."

"We had lunch, too. Daddy got me bows for my hair." Zoe bent her head and showed off two glitter-laden pink bows.

"You look so sparkly."

Zoe grinned.

"Now I need you to go up to your room for a little while with your cookbook and let me talk to your daddy."

"Yes, Mommy." She turned to Reece and offered him a bear hug. "Thank you. Thank you."

Reece leaned against the counter, hands tucked into his jeans and his blue cotton dress shirt rolled up at the sleeves. "What's wrong?" His brows were furrowed with concern. "Is it Asa?"

"No." She sank back into a chair and pushed the letter across the table.

Reece sat down and quickly skimmed the contents. He ran a hand over his face and shook his head. "I mentioned the draft custody agreement to you when I said I talked to my attorney and he recommended the back child support. Remember?"

"Maybe. But that seems like a long time ago and I don't know what I remember at this point."

"Look this is about my attorney's billable

hours. I talked to him about Zoe in June and asked him to hold for a couple of months. I don't know why it was sent. I'm sorry."

"I've been functioning on a one-day-at-a-time mentality for the last eight weeks or so and you've been taking the long view. I guess that hasn't changed has it?" She swallowed, stunned that that this was today's discussion. The day had begun with so much hope.

"Will you seek to be the primary custodian, leaving me with every other weekend, half the holidays and half the summer?" she asked. "Or do you plan to take everything from me?"

Tense stillness filled the room and Claire dared to meet his gaze, almost afraid of the truth she might see in his eyes.

"Claire," he began, his voice steely and emotionless. "Let me caution you. Words have so much power. They are what kept me from my daughter for five years. I said things that I regret and lost you and Zoe. Take some time to process. Then we can talk."

"What's to process? I received a letter informing me that you're ready to move forward with a custody battle. You should have talked to me before you talked to your attorney."

"When I found out Zoe was my daughter, you and I weren't really talking much. I met with my attorney and then the whole thing was on the back burner. I've been pretty busy since then managing two businesses and trying to become a father to my daughter."

"Still you didn't answer my question."

"And I'm not going to. Things have changed since June. You and I have changed since June."

Pain squeezed her heart and she grimaced.

"Are you okay?" he asked.

"No. I'm not." She took slow breaths, willing herself to calm down. So many times the people she loved walked away or were taken away. She couldn't handle it one more time.

"I trusted you," she murmured. Trusted him and fell in love with him again, despite every precaution she'd taken not to. Yet, there it was.

"No, you didn't." His expression darkened. "You trusted your belief that I would let you down like everyone else. You've been waiting for it, expecting my betrayal every single day." He shook his head.

Silence filled the room for long minutes before he spoke again.

"I think you and I need a little breather."

"What's that supposed to mean?" she asked.

"It means that I was about to send Mitch out of town to meet with an important potential customer for the ranch, but I'll go. It's my job, and I guess I forgot that." He wrapped one hand around the other. "I'll be flying out to Denver on Sunday."

"You're leaving."

"I'll be at the ceremony on Saturday. Because I promised. If you need anything—"

"I don't need a thing. Not a thing."

He took a deep breath and released a sigh. "If Zoe needs anything, Violet at the front desk has the itinerary." Reece stood and turned to go. Then he looked back.

"You know, Claire, something's been gnawing at me all these weeks."

She raised her head, prepared for the worst.

"Why didn't you ever tell Davis that I'm Zoe's father? Were you ashamed of me?"

Claire lowered her gaze to the letter at the table. "I was ashamed of myself. Ashamed that I fell in love with someone who didn't love me back."

The sound of the door closing filled the empty room.

When Zoe skipped into the kitchen, Claire was still staring blankly at the door.

"Where's my daddy?" Zoe asked, confusion on her face.

"He had to go."

"Is he coming back?"

Claire closed her eyes and searched for the words, the right words, for Zoe. She couldn't find them.

Chapter Ten

Claire stood stiffly on the small stage, looking out at all the people in Rebel who loved and respected her father. She white-knuckled the wooden podium, willing her legs to stop shaking and her stomach to settle down. Emotion rolled over her in waves as she concluded the speech that she had practiced over and over again in the mirror this week.

"Every time I visit Rebel, I'll be reminded of how much this town meant to my father and how he treasured the citizens. His friends and neighbors. Thank you for this honor."

The applause in the auditorium echoed, the effect overwhelming. Claire took a deep breath and her gaze scanned the room, taking in those in attendance. The Rainbolts, the Turners, Pastor and Saylor Tuttle filled the first few rows. Daisy was right. The Rainbolts were multiplying.

She avoided making eye contact with Reece, though he, too, sat in the front row with Zoe next to him.

When the mayor stepped forward and pulled the draping off the bronze plaque that would be placed in the community center foyer, another round of applause ensued.

Then it was over. She was back in the same place she had been in April when she buried her father. Chilled to the bone and making benign small talk as her heart broke into little pieces.

Claire glanced at the clock in the reception hall and calculated when it would be polite to slip out.

"I saw that," Daisy said as she sidled close.

"Don't tell anyone."

"Our secret." She offered a sympathetic smile. "And my guess is that you have about thirty minutes more."

"Best news I've heard all day."

"Claire, do you mind if I ask you a personal question?"

"Daisy, you don't usually ask first."

"That is true." The redhead smiled. "You mentioned visiting Rebel in your speech. Are you leaving?"

"That's really always been the plan. I have a job in Tulsa. Zoe starts school in two weeks."

"What about Reece?"

"Maybe we can chat later this week," Claire said.

"You're right, I'm sorry. This really isn't the time."

"Mommy, may I have cake?"

"Let me take care of that for you," Daisy said. "Come on, Zoe. Let's go see which cake looks best."

"What kind is there?"

"Lemon and coconut, and I made them both so it's going to be hard to decide."

Claire scanned the room once again, but there was no sign of Reece. Nan approached from across the room. "Nan, thank you for coming."

"It was real nice. Had me missing Davis all over again."

"Tell me about it."

Nan put an arm around Claire's shoulders. "Oh, I'm so sorry. Of course, this has been hard on you. It's only been four months. I know you're missing him."

"I never really understood until now how grief works. It strikes whenever it pleases, doesn't it?"

"Sadly, yes." Nan nodded. "Hang in there."

"I will."

"We're heading out. Asa is ready to go. He can only tolerate being on his feet for so long."

"Is there anything I can do?"

"Once he's in his recliner, the pain is manageable." Nan cocked her head and hesitated for a beat. "Honey, is there something going on between you and Reece?"

"Why do you ask?"

"I just saw him leave. He looked like a man who lost his best friend, and he hugged Zoe like he'd never see her again. I got the definite impression that something was wrong."

"I don't think I'm ready to talk about Reece." She wasn't sure she'd ever be ready.

"I'm here if you need me."

"I'll be fine," Claire murmured.

"Spoken like a true Ballard." Nan clucked her tongue and offered a sad smile. "Except that strategy didn't work out too well for your father and I expect it isn't working out too well for you."

"Nan, you've been around us way too long. You know all our foibles."

"Let me give you my best unsolicited advice. You're a nurse. Give yourself the same compassion you give your patients."

"Meaning?"

"Don't be so hard on yourself."

"But I keep making the same mistakes."

"Things are going to work out. God has a plan. Maybe you can get out of the driver's seat for a little bit and let Him show you what He has in mind."

"I know you're right. I do need to get out of my own way." If only she could.

Thirty minutes later, she began to make the rounds, saying good-night and thanking the mayor and the town council members for the honor they'd bestowed upon her father's memory. By the time she was in the car and headed home, she was numb.

She went through the motions, taking Blue out for a walk, getting Zoe ready for bed and reading to her. Finally, the house was quiet and she sat at the kitchen table with a cup of coffee, thinking.

When the doorbell rang, she froze. Reece? Surely not. Could she dare hope she had a second chance to make things right? Did she even know how to?

Claire opened the door and found Willard on her doorstep.

"Sorry to bother you, Ms. Ballard, but I saw your light was still on and Reece asked me to run this over to you when I had a minute."

He handed her an envelope and released a dramatic sigh.

"Everything all right, Willard?"

"No, ma'am, it surely is not. The world is all off-kilter and there doesn't seem to be a thing I can do about it." He tipped his hat. "If you need anything, anything at all, you give a call over to the ranch and I'll be over in a jiffy."

"Thank you."

Closing the door behind him, she tossed the

envelope on the table. There were far too many envelopes in her life lately and too few of them helped her sleep at night. She walked away from the table and reheated her coffee in the microwave. Leaning against the counter, sipping from the mug, she stared at it for several minutes. Finally, she snatched the envelope and ripped it open.

A check slipped out. That was all. A check. The subject line read, *For the purchase of one-half of Ballard Farm.*

Stunned, Claire turned the check over, examining the paper from all angles. Reece's bold signature revealed nothing.

Claire released a breath. Instead of satisfaction, or even relief, anger surged.

Reece Rainbolt had pulled the rug out from under her for the second time in a lifetime and she absolutely refused to let him get away with it again.

It was as if a lightbulb went off. They were two cowards and it had to stop for their daughter's sake. Zoe would be the collateral damage because they were both too proud and too afraid to compromise and stake a claim.

Like her mother and her father who had retreated into their comfort zones rather than fight for what they wanted, both Claire and Reece walked away when the going got tough.

Claire absolutely refused let that happen again. She was going to fight for what she wanted and what her daughter deserved.

"Tell me again why you're going to Denver, instead of Mitch," Willard said. His arms were loped over the top of the fence as he watched Reece give his horse a cooldown.

Reece clamped his jaw as he recalled Claire's speech in the community center. *Every time I visit Rebel.*

"You ignoring me?" Willard persisted.

"I've been running my life without a mother or a father for a very long time," Reece said. He shot Willard a steady glare that the old cowboy ignored as usual.

"They say that when you find yourself in a hole, the first thing to do is stop digging."

Reece straightened and wiped the August humidity off his brow. "What are you jawing about?"

"Ever since you handed me that envelope to drop off at Ballard Farm, I can't help but notice that your attitude could use an adjustment."

"I don't pay you to notice my attitude." He met Willard's gaze. "I guess you forgot that I'm the boss."

"To tell you the truth, I have so many people I

call boss around here it doesn't really matter if I have one more or one less."

Reece ran a hand over the horse's withers and shook his head. "Trust me, it will matter when you pick up your paycheck."

"No one here but you and me. Maybe you want to get what's bothering you off your chest."

"Now you're offering therapy?"

Willard shrugged. "Maybe a little wisdom. I've made plenty of mistakes and it couldn't hurt for you to avoid a couple, two or three, before your regrets start piling up."

A long shadow covered the yard in front of the barn and Reece looked up at the sky. "That's not good."

"Yep. The forecast says clouds moving in today with a chance of precipitation come Wednesday. Summer's almost over."

Yeah, summer was almost over. A lot of things were almost over. Reece glanced at his watch and then pointedly at Willard. "I've got to go pack. Can you finish this for me?"

"Surely. Happy to, boss."

"Thanks." Reece started to walk toward the house.

"Why do you suppose you're taking the last plane out of town tonight and you haven't packed?"

"I'm guessing you're going to tell me," Reece said without stopping.

"Maybe you're hoping Claire will call and you won't have to go."

Reece turned around and took a deep breath. "What is it you think you know, Cornell?"

"I know that you're in love with Claire and Zoe and you've got too much pride to fight for them."

Reece clenched his fists and stared the old cowboy down.

"Well, I guess I'll take care of the horse now," Willard said with a hasty step in the other direction.

Swiveling on his boot heel, Reece stomped to the house, praying nothing stopped him before he got inside.

He tossed his suitcase on the bed and threw his clothes inside. Willard Cornell didn't know what he was talking about. It didn't matter how Reece felt about Claire. She didn't need him except as a contingency plan.

A safety net. Because she didn't have the courage to choose to trust him. To step out in faith. Not six years ago and not now.

Nope, it wasn't because he'd shot off his big mouth about not wanting a relationship back then. It was because he was a wild card and she wanted all her i's dotted. Claire claimed to have fallen in love with him then but what did it matter if she was still afraid to commit to anything beyond today and she was still ready to believe the worst of him.

On Wednesday, Reece was still fuming about Willard as he sat in a conference room for his third meeting of the day. He hadn't slept in three nights and he was restless and agitated.

He glanced at the weather app on his phone and grimaced. Strong winds and rain had moved into Osage County. The storm was moving heavy and fast just as Ballard Farm was scheduled to harvest the next round of peaches, start on the early apples and plant the pecan cover crops.

"Everything all right there, Mr. Rainbolt?"

"Some bad weather back home." His phone began to buzz.

"Do you need to take that?"

"I do, sir, if you don't mind." He nodded in apology and stepped outside of the room.

Willard's voice boomed over the phone. "Boss, I got news, and I got news."

"Okay."

"It's raining here and we have some heavy winds moving through. That big tree out back just hit the Ballard Farm's market building. They're without electricity and a front door. The greenhouses took a hit, too."

Reece tensed. Zoe and Claire worked in the

market building with Nan on occasion. "Was anyone… Are Claire and Zoe all right?"

"Yeah. Everyone is fine. They shut things down when the sky got dark."

Relief was swift, and then Reece began to blame himself. He'd absently noticed that tree was mostly dead weeks ago. It should have been removed then.

"What's the good news?" he asked Willard.

"Who said there was good news?"

"Okay." Reece paused, thinking. "Call and get someone out there to deal with that tree."

"Not gonna happen. We've got downed power lines and everyone else is dealing with their own tree damage."

"Is it still raining?"

"Off and on. I'm headed over there to help bring in the late peaches, if it stops raining anytime soon."

"I'll change my flight and be there after lunch."

"I knew you wouldn't let Claire down."

"I don't want Claire to know I'm coming home early to help. I mean it. Keep your lips sealed if you want to stay employed."

"I don't see what the big deal is."

Yeah, and Reece didn't either, but he suspected Claire would find some ulterior motive in his early return. Somehow he'd have to prove to her what he was only just beginning to admit to himself. That he cared. Far more than he'd realized when he boarded the plane for Denver.

"You hear me, Cornell?"

"You remind me an awful lot of Mitch before he figured out why every time he ran his head into a brick wall it hurt. Daisy was very patient."

"Did you hear what I said? Say nothing."

"I surely will not, because I want to be around when the 'I told you sos' are passed out. I'll be first in line to collect mine."

Reece hung up the phone and tried to figure out a few good reasons why he shouldn't fire Willard right now. The only thing that stood between the old cowboy and a pink slip was that he was right. And that was what annoyed Reece most of all.

"It wasn't supposed to rain all day." Claire stood at the entrance of the barn, looking out at the sheets of water. It had been raining for eight hours. She shivered beneath her slicker.

"Did you call over to Rebel Ranch?" Nan asked.

"I called Willard. He's going to bring someone to get that tree off the market building as soon as it stops raining."

"We'll have to hustle and get those peaches harvested once the rain stops. Can't let the ripe fruit sit on the branches. Fungus is a threat."

"Nan, the part-time workers have gone back to college. We haven't had much response from the hiring ads. I wasn't too worried because it wasn't supposed to rain like this."

"Are you saying it's just us?"

"It's a skeleton crew this week."

"What about Reece?"

"Reece is out of town." Out of town and out of her life because she'd jumped to conclusions.

"Half of the farm is his, so you probably have an obligation to notify him that we're having some problems over here."

Half the farm. All of the farm, if Claire decided to cash the check that had been folded and stuffed into her Bible. It was right next to the verse Nan had quoted in *Lamentations*. *His compassions fail not.*

Well, she was trusting that His compassion would not fail. Trusting as she had never before in her life that somehow, someway, things would be fixed and she would never have to cash that check.

Thunder boomed, shaking the rafters of the barn.

"Did you hear me, Claire? I think we should call Reece."

Claire crossed her arms. "Nan, I was raised here. Everyone keeps saying that I can handle the farm, so why is it Reece's name keeps coming up when we're between a rock and a hard place?"

"You're right, of course, dear. However, I think Reece might have a bit more experience with a rock and a hard place, that's all."

Claire bit back a smile at the older woman's diplomacy.

"Is that a truck in the drive?" Nan asked moments later.

"Yes, those are headlights," Claire said. The vehicle parked and two figures approached through the pelting rain.

"Well, look who's here," Nan said.

Claire stared as Reece and Willard ran up the drive and ducked into the open barn. When the door was pushed open, she was nearly knocked to the ground. She stumbled back and a hand reached out to grab her arm and keep her from landing on her backside.

"Whoa. Sorry about that," Reece said.

For a moment, she could only stare at him, her emotions in turmoil. How could she be as annoyed as she was happy to see the man?

"What are you doing here?" she asked.

"Good to see you, too, Claire," he murmured.

Okay, it *was* good to see him. She hadn't seen him in four days. Though, that was beside the point. "You were in Denver," she accused.

"Hour and a half flight. Had to come back to check on my farm."

Of course, his farm. That was the only reason he returned.

"It's only half your farm," she said.

He frowned and leaned closer. "Didn't you get my check?"

"I have no plans to cash that check and let you off the hook," she whispered.

Reece jerked back in stunned surprise. "That's the first good thing I've heard in a week." He turned to Willard. "Let's go assess the damage from that fallen tree and see how the greenhouses fared."

"It's raining out there," Willard whined.

Reece turned to Claire. "I've got a friend with equipment that will help us get it off the building. In the meantime, maybe you can order a tent we can use for produce sales."

Claire crossed her arms and met his gaze. "I already ordered it and I assessed the greenhouses, as well. Minimal damage to a few panels, but we have replacement supplies."

A smile lit his lips and he offered a nod of respect. Then he turned to Nan. "How's Asa?"

"Stable. Thanks for asking."

He looked up at the sky. "Rain should move out tonight. Mitch and Tucker will be by first thing in the morning and we'll get those peaches moving."

"Wonderful. Claire and I are going to pick when it slows to a drizzle."

"You pick in the rain?" he asked.

"It's actually kind of fun," Nan said.

Reece looked around and then met Claire's gaze. "Where's Zoe?"

"She's at Daisy's."

He nodded and again leaned closer. "We're going to talk."

"Oh, you can count on it," she said. They were going to talk and this time she wasn't going to let either one of them off the hook.

The rain was only spitting water by late afternoon when Reece showed up at the back door. Claire stood at the screen. She'd been waiting for him, practicing what she was going to say, praying and pacing the floor.

Her future rested in how the next minutes played out and yet when she saw him approach, she found herself tongue-tied.

"There's a rainbow," she finally said.

He turned and glanced up at the sky where the clouds had parted to reveal a hazy arc of color. "I guess we don't have to build an ark, after all."

"I guess not."

"May I come in?" he asked.

She pushed open the screen door. "Coffee?"

"I've had my share today, thanks." Expression

solemn, he shrugged off his jacket and placed it on the doorknob. "Mind if I sit down?"

Claire gestured toward the chair.

"You really didn't need my help today," Reece said. You had everything under control."

"Did I?" she asked.

"You know you did. You're your father's daughter and I'm pretty sure you could run the entire farm yourself if you wanted."

The words were a balm to her ears, but they didn't solve the problem at hand.

"Except that I don't want to manage the farm myself." She sat down and pulled her Bible toward her. Flipping the pages, she pulled out the check and slid it across the table. "I don't want this either. Thanks for the offer, but I officially decline."

He arched a brow. "You asked for this in June. Remember?"

"I remember. But June was a long time ago, and as it turns out, I was wrong."

"What do you want, Claire?"

"I want to apologize to you, first." She studied the pattern of the tabletop and then raised her eyes to his. The dark blue eyes were cautious as they met hers. "And I want a second chance, Reece."

"Does that mean you believe me about the attorney?"

"I tore the letter in half and mailed it back to him."

"You did?"

"Yes." She cleared her throat and looked at him sitting across the table from her as she struggled to find the courage to say the words that needed to be said.

"Look. You were right. I put myself in a no-win situation. If I accepted that you had changed and allowed myself to care for you, I was at risk of letting my heart get broken again. It was much safer to deny how I really felt about you."

"Which is?"

"I'm in love with you, Reece." Her heart pounded in her chest as she said the words. Simple words, really. Nothing complicated about them, yet they could close the door on the past and open another one to the future. Her life hung precariously on his response.

"What about your nursing job?" he asked.

"I've put in twelve years. It's time for a career change."

"Would you consider being a farmer's wife?"

Claire blinked and her head shot up at the words. "What?"

"Long-range view." A small smile touched his lips. "I want to be very clear this time. I love you, Claire."

Her chest tightened with happiness, but she

held back. She had to be absolutely certain. "You love me, or do you love Zoe's mother?"

"Claire, I loved you long before I loved Zoe."

"You did?"

"Haven't I shown you that this summer? I've all but abandoned Rebel Ranch to be where you are. Everything about you brightens my day. I thought I was doing fine all this time. But when you came back to Rebel in June, I realized I've only been going through the motions. You opened the shutters on my life again."

"Why did you leave Denver?" she asked.

"The storm gave me a reason to come home to fight for us, Claire."

"You wouldn't have come otherwise?"

"Sure I would have. But as Willard likes to point out, I can be pigheaded and it might have taken longer if that tree hadn't fallen down and I wasn't worried about you."

"Someone once told me that I'm literal. That I like to have things spelled out."

"That I can do." Reece smiled as he reached for her notebook. He flipped through all the pages filled with lists until he found a blank page. In large letters, he wrote, *I love you, Claire Ballard.*

Claire sucked in a breath at the words, her hands moving to her mouth as emotion filled her eyes and her heart ached with joy.

He tore out the page and came around the table.

Getting down on one knee, he handed the paper to her.

"Claire," he breathed before his lips touched hers in a kiss that erased all doubt. Reece loved her.

When he lifted his head, Claire blinked. "I must be dreaming."

"Good. Make sure you dream big."

Epilogue

"Coffee?"

Claire dragged her eyes away from the view of Rebel Ranch from Reece's patio. She could see all the way to the redbud trees whose leaves had already begun to turn a bright canary yellow as September faded into October.

"Yes, please. Thank you."

When Reece bent down to press a kiss to her forehead, she could only sigh and send up a prayer of thanks to God. It had taken Reece's unconditional love and patience to give them a second chance.

"I could get used to this," she said.

"I think that's the reason we got married. That, and the fact that I love you." He leaned against the stone rail and sipped his coffee, silhouetted by the last traces of a rosy sunrise dissolving into the new day.

"I thought you married me for Ballard Farm." Claire held up her hand and admired the wedding set on her left hand. They hadn't wasted any time in making it official. No, they had already wasted six long years.

He snorted. "Yeah, not hardly."

She could only chuckle.

"What do you want to do about your father's house?" Reece asked.

"I've been giving that some serious thought. Did you know that there is only one bed-and-breakfast in Rebel? The nearest hotel is in Hominy."

"Rebel Ranch. Guest ranch? Remember?"

"Yes, there is that."

"What did you have in mind?"

"What do you think about Ballard Farm Bed-and-Breakfast?" She swept a hand through the air. "Doesn't that have a nice ring to it?"

"You'll be in direct competition with Rebel Ranch." He frowned and shook his head.

"No. It's apples and peaches." She laughed. "Pun intended."

"You're hanging around Willard too much."

"Oh, you're just annoyed because he said I told you so a couple dozen times."

"Enough about Willard. You were saying?"

"I was saying that my B&B will offer one experience and Rebel Ranch offers a different one. I see my business catering to a more mature clientele. As long as we target our specific demographics, then it's a win-win for both of us."

"I'm all for win-win. In fact, I'm living a win-win."

"Aw, that's so sweet."

"Thank you. And now that the business portion of this honeymoon is over, what's on our agenda for today, Madam Entrepreneur?"

She smiled, knowing she would never tire of hearing him say *our*.

"It's our last day. What about a picnic up at the creek? Then we can pick up Zoe from Daisy and Mitch's."

"I'd like that. By the way, I promised Zoe I'd discuss something with you."

"What's that?"

"She'd like a brother or sister. There is no preference. Either will do."

"Reece, you cannot promise a five-year-old a brother or sister." Claire found herself unable to stop laughing. "You Rainbolts are aiming to raise the population of Rebel single-handedly."

He offered a mischievous smile. "I wouldn't exactly say single-handedly."

Claire laughed again.

"Can we discuss the idea?" he asked.

"Yes. We can, however, I think we should provide a united front in letting Zoe know that she'll get a brother or sister in God's timing."

"I like that, and it sounds like co-parenting. We're getting really good at that, aren't we?"

Claire put her coffee down and stood. She walked to her husband and put her arms around his neck, pulling his head down to hers.

"I love you, Reece Rainbolt, and I don't want to ever co-parent with anyone but you."

She closed her eyes as he kissed her forehead, her nose and finally her lips. When he raised his head and met her gaze, love shined bright in the dark blue eyes.

"I love you, too, Claire Ballard-Rainbolt."

* * * * *

If you enjoyed this story,
don't miss the next book
in Tina Radcliffe's Hearts of Oklahoma series,
available later this year from Love Inspired!

Find more great reads at
www.LoveInspired.com.

Dear Reader,

Welcome back to Rebel, Oklahoma. Once a working cattle ranch, Rebel Ranch is now a guest ranch owned by the Rainbolt siblings, Mitch, Reece, Tucker and Kate.

The second book in the series is a journey about forgiveness, trust and second chances. It's Reece Rainbolt and Claire Ballard's story about the power of God's unconditional love.

It's always my pleasure to mix faith with laughter in my stories, because I serve a God who clearly has a sense of humor.

Please do email me and let me know your thoughts. I can be reached through my website, www.tinaradcliffe.com. You can also find my family's Christmas cookie recipes there. Happy reading.

Sincerely,
Tina Radcliffe

Get 4 FREE REWARDS!

We'll send you 2 FREE Books plus 2 FREE Mystery Gifts.

Love Inspired Suspense books showcase how courage and optimism unite in stories of faith and love in the face of danger.

FREE Value Over **$20**

YES! Please send me 2 FREE Love Inspired Suspense novels and my 2 FREE mystery gifts (gifts are worth about $10 retail). After receiving them, if I don't wish to receive any more books, I can return the shipping statement marked "cancel." If I don't cancel, I will receive 6 brand-new novels every month and be billed just $5.24 each for the regular-print edition or $5.99 each for the larger-print edition in the U.S., or $5.74 each for the regular-print edition or $6.24 each for the larger-print edition in Canada. That's a savings of at least 13% off the cover price. It's quite a bargain! Shipping and handling is just 50¢ per book in the U.S. and $1.25 per book in Canada.* I understand that accepting the 2 free books and gifts places me under no obligation to buy anything. I can always return a shipment and cancel at any time. The free books and gifts are mine to keep no matter what I decide.

Choose one: ☐ **Love Inspired Suspense** ☐ **Love Inspired Suspense**
　　　　　　　Regular-Print　　　　　　　　**Larger-Print**
　　　　　　　(153/353 IDN GNWN)　　　　　(107/307 IDN GNWN)

Name (please print)

Address   Apt. #

City   State/Province   Zip/Postal Code

Email: Please check this box ☐ if you would like to receive newsletters and promotional emails from Harlequin Enterprises ULC and its affiliates. You can unsubscribe anytime.

Mail to the **Reader Service:**
IN U.S.A.: P.O. Box 1341, Buffalo, NY 14240-8531
IN CANADA: P.O. Box 603, Fort Erie, Ontario L2A 5X3

Want to try 2 free books from another series? Call 1-800-873-8635 or visit www.ReaderService.com.

*Terms and prices subject to change without notice. Prices do not include sales taxes, which will be charged (if applicable) based on your state or country of residence. Canadian residents will be charged applicable taxes. Offer not valid in Quebec. This offer is limited to one order per household. Books received may not be as shown. Not valid for current subscribers to Love Inspired Suspense books. All orders subject to approval. Credit or debit balances in a customer's account(s) may be offset by any other outstanding balance owed by or to the customer. Please allow 4 to 6 weeks for delivery. Offer available while quantities last.

Your Privacy—Your information is being collected by Harlequin Enterprises ULC, operating as Reader Service. For a complete summary of the information we collect, how we use this information and to whom it is disclosed, please visit our privacy notice located at corporate.harlequin.com/privacy-notice. From time to time we may also exchange your personal information with reputable third parties. If you wish to opt out of this sharing of your personal information, please visit readerservice.com/consumerschoice or call 1-800-873-8635. **Notice to California Residents**—Under California law, you have specific rights to control and access your data. For more information on these rights and how to exercise them, visit corporate.harlequin.com/california-privacy.

LIS20R2

Get 4 FREE REWARDS!

We'll send you 2 FREE Books
<u>plus</u> 2 FREE Mystery Gifts.

Harlequin Heartwarming Larger-Print books will connect you to uplifting stories where the bonds of friendship, family and community unite.

FREE Value Over **$20**

YES! Please send me 2 FREE Harlequin Heartwarming Larger-Print novels and my 2 FREE mystery gifts (gifts worth about $10 retail). After receiving them, if I don't wish to receive any more books, I can return the shipping statement marked "cancel." If I don't cancel, I will receive 4 brand-new larger-print novels every month and be billed just $5.74 per book in the U.S. or $6.24 per book in Canada. That's a savings of at least 21% off the cover price. It's quite a bargain! Shipping and handling is just 50¢ per book in the U.S. and $1.25 per book in Canada.* I understand that accepting the 2 free books and gifts places me under no obligation to buy anything. I can always return a shipment and cancel at any time. The free books and gifts are mine to keep no matter what I decide.

161/361 HDN GNPZ

Name (please print)

Address   Apt. #

City   State/Province   Zip/Postal Code

Email: Please check this box ☐ if you would like to receive newsletters and promotional emails from Harlequin Enterprises ULC and its affiliates. You can unsubscribe anytime.

Mail to the **Reader Service:**
IN U.S.A.: P.O. Box 1341, Buffalo, NY 14240-8531
IN CANADA: P.O. Box 603, Fort Erie, Ontario L2A 5X3

Want to try 2 free books from another series! Call 1-800-873-8635 or visit www.ReaderService.com.

---

*Terms and prices subject to change without notice. Prices do not include sales taxes, which will be charged (if applicable) based on your state or country of residence. Canadian residents will be charged applicable taxes. Offer not valid in Quebec. This offer is limited to one order per household. Books received may not be as shown. Not valid for current subscribers to Harlequin Heartwarming Larger-Print books. All orders subject to approval. Credit or debit balances in a customer's account(s) may be offset by any other outstanding balance owed by or to the customer. Please allow 4 to 6 weeks for delivery. Offer available while quantities last.

Your Privacy—Your information is being collected by Harlequin Enterprises ULC, operating as Reader Service. For a complete summary of the information we collect, how we use this information and to whom it is disclosed, please visit our privacy notice located at corporate.harlequin.com/privacy-notice. From time to time we may also exchange your personal information with reputable third parties. If you wish to opt out of this sharing of your personal information, please visit readerservice.com/consumerschoice or call 1-800-873-8635. **Notice to California Residents**—Under California law, you have specific rights to control and access your data. For more information on these rights and how to exercise them, visit corporate.harlequin.com/california-privacy.

HW20R2

THE WESTERN HEARTS COLLECTION!

19 FREE BOOKS in all!

COWBOYS. RANCHERS. RODEO REBELS.
Here are their charming love stories in one prized Collection:
51 emotional and heart-filled romances that capture the majesty and rugged beauty of the American West!

YES! Please send me **The Western Hearts Collection** in Larger Print. This collection begins with 3 FREE books and 2 FREE gifts in the first shipment. Along with my 3 free books, I'll also get the next 4 books from The Western Hearts Collection, in LARGER PRINT, which I may either return and owe nothing, or keep for the low price of $5.45 U.S./$6.23 CDN each plus $2.99 U.S./$7.49 CDN for shipping and handling per shipment*. If I decide to continue, about once a month for 8 months I will get 6 or 7 more books but will only need to pay for 4. That means 2 or 3 books in every shipment will be FREE! If I decide to keep the entire collection, I'll have paid for only 32 books because 19 books are FREE! I understand that accepting the 3 free books and gifts places me under no obligation to buy anything. I can always return a shipment and cancel at any time. My free books and gifts are mine to keep no matter what I decide.

☐ 270 HCN 5354   ☐ 470 HCN 5354

Name (please print)

Address   Apt. #

City   State/Province   Zip/Postal Code

Mail to the Reader Service:
IN U.S.A.: P.O. Box 1341, Buffalo, N.Y. 14240-8531
IN CANADA: P.O. Box 603, Fort Erie, Ontario L2A 5X3

*Terms and prices subject to change without notice. Prices do not include sales taxes, which will be charged (if applicable) based on your state or country of residence. Canadian residents will be charged applicable taxes. Offer not valid in Quebec. All orders subject to approval. Credit or debit balances in a customer's account(s) may be offset by any other outstanding balance owed by or to the customer. Please allow three to four weeks for delivery. Offer available while quantities last. © 2020 Harlequin Enterprises ULC. ® and ™ are trademarks owned by Harlequin Enterprises ULC.

Your Privacy—The Reader Service is committed to protecting your privacy. Our Privacy Policy is available online at www.ReaderService.com or upon request from the Reader Service. We make a portion of our mailing list available to reputable third parties that offer products we believe may interest you. If you prefer that we not exchange your name with third parties, or if you wish to clarify or modify your communication preferences, please visit us at www.ReaderService.com/consumerschoice or write to us at Reader Service Mail Preference Service, P.O. Box 9062, Buffalo, NY 14269. Include your complete name and address.

50BWH20